A Goal in Sight

This book is dedicated to The Calgary Seeing Ice Dogs

A real hockey team with a real hockey dream!

The Calgary Seeing Ice Dogs

Blind Players:
Jeff Galbraith #14 — Right Forward
Al Laughlin #9 — Left Forward
Randy Cameron #47 — Center
Rod Rogalsky #16 — Center
Brian Clark #22 — Goalie/Forward
Gary Zarbock #33 — Goalie

Sighted Players and Volunteers:
Kevin Gardner #12 — Defence
Rob Lane #19 — Defence
Danny Dawes #10 — Defence
Dale Richardson #11 — Forward
Ian Richardson #7 — Defence
Brandon Van Dyk #4 — Defence
Andy Clark #66 — Defence
Bill Galbraith — Volunteer/Co-ordinator
Dee Van Dyk — Support Staff

A Goal in Sight

Jacqueline Guest

James Lorimer & Company Ltd., Publishers
Toronto, 2002

James Lorimer & Company Ltd. acknowledges the support of the Ontario Arts Council. We acknowledge the support of the Government of Canada, through the Book Publishing Industry Development Program (BPIDP), for our publishing activities.

We acknowledge the support of the Canada Council for the Arts for our publishing program.

Cover illustration: Maurice Bernard

National Library of Canada Cataloguing in Publication Data

Guest, Jacqueline
    A goal in sight / Jacqueline Guest.

(Sports stories)
ISBN 1-55028-779-6 (bound). — ISBN 1-55028-780-X (pbk.)

    I. Title. II. Series: Sports stories (Toronto, Ont.)

| PS8563.U365G62 2002 | jC813'.54 | C2002-904279-8 |
| PZ7 | | |

James Lorimer & Company Limited, Publishers	Distributed in the United States by:
35 Britain Street	Orca Book Publishers
Toronto, Ontario	P.O. Box 468
M5A 1R7	Custer, WA USA
www.lorimer.ca	98240-0468

Printed and bound in Canada

Contents

1

Life Sucks!

Aiden Walsh timed his strike perfectly. Gripping his hockey stick tightly with both hands, he lined up his target in his sights and went in for the kill. The kid never knew what hit him. The guy hit the boards with a satisfying *whump*, then went down onto the ice.

The ref's whistle blew before Aiden had taken half a stride.

Aiden didn't bother looking at the ref. He knew he'd drawn a five-minute major for cross-checking but he didn't care. He'd taken the Springhill Rangers' lead scorer out. He knew the coach would keep the guy on the bench for a couple of shifts to recover and with so little time left in the game, that's all Aiden's team, the Oakridge Devils, would need. They were in the lead and now, they would keep it. The rest of the Rangers were next to useless at goal scoring and posed no threat.

Here in Calgary, Alberta, everyone knew Aiden Walsh was the toughest defenceman in the league and the Devils were winners because of it.

Aiden glided over to the penalty box. He wouldn't have much time once he'd sat out his stupid penalty, but he wanted to nuke one more guy before the end of the game. He scanned the ice for the irritating forward. The kid's jersey advertised him as *Walberg 33*. He was fast and way too accurate with his shots.

The annoying winger was the only remaining Ranger who might be a threat to the Devils' lead.

Walberg had also checked him hard, sending Aiden into the boards and that was something Aiden couldn't let the guy get away with. He had a reputation to uphold. They'd been dicing all game and Aiden wanted to teach the guy a real lesson about messing with the Devils…and Aiden Walsh.

Anxiously, he watched the action on the ice. He was itching to get back out there. He always hated having to waste precious minutes in the penalty box, but that was all part of playing tough hockey. Looking up into the stands behind the Devils' bench, Aiden saw his dad, Charlie, in his usual seat.

Aiden had always called his dad Charlie, which suited the big man more than *Daddy* or *Father*. Charlie wasn't the kind of guy who liked soft and fuzzy.

Charlie waved at Aiden and gave the thumbs-up sign, then pounded his fist into the palm of his hand. This was their signal that it was a great hit and his dad really approved. Aiden grinned back and nodded his head.

His dad pointed to a Ranger player on the ice. It was Walberg 33. Charlie had apparently spotted him as a problem as well. Aiden watched the skater for a moment, then nodded his head at his dad, agreeing. All he needed was a couple of minutes to set up his run at his final target of the game.

"Try to spend more time on the ice than in the penalty box, Aiden!" Jamie Cook, the Devils' captain, called as he skated past.

"You do your job, Cook, and I'll do mine," Aiden yelled back, keeping his eyes on the Ranger forward. He and Jamie used to be friends, but lately they hadn't been getting along very well. The guy should make up his mind what he wanted. Aiden's tactics had never been questioned before. He was the

Devils' muscle and he'd always done a great job at taking out players who got in the way of a win. Sure he took a lot of penalties, but that was part of it.

"I'm trying, but I need all my players to be on the same side!" Jamie called over his shoulder.

Aiden shook his head, irritated. Jamie was referring to earlier in the game when, while trying to crush one of the opposition into the boards, Aiden had miscalculated and bounced Steven Becker, the Devils' forward, instead. Accidents happen. It wasn't his fault Steven hadn't been fast enough in getting out of the way!

After what seemed like forever, the penalty box timekeeper released him. He hit the ice with his skates on fire. Walberg 33 was at the other end of rink in his own zone. Aiden circled the far side of the ice, ignoring the puck action and zeroing in on his target.

The forward saw him coming and headed back down to the Devils' end. Aiden started picking up speed, calculating just where he would take him out. He was totally focused.

The shrill of the buzzer signalling the end of the game made Aiden's head snap up. He thought he had a couple more minutes and that's all he would have needed. The Devils had won 6-3. That meant the Devils were closing in on first place in the Calgary Minor Hockey League, something the team had never done before. He spotted Walberg skating toward the Rangers' bench and debated on whether he should take him out anyway, but decided he could wait until their next game together.

Aiden lined up with the other players to shake hands. He noticed a lot of the Ranger players didn't want to shake his hand, but he didn't care. They weren't important; they were losers…6-3 losers!

After changing, Aiden headed out to the parking lot to wait

for his dad to pull up in their old Chevy truck. He looked up at the night sky. Large flakes of snow were softly falling out of the darkness. He could feel them land on his eyelashes and cheeks. Soft, cold, powdered ice. He blinked to clear his vision, noticing two Springhill Ranger players coming out of the arena.

One was a big defenceman he'd tripped in the first period; the other was Walberg 33. Aiden straightened up, his fists curling into useable weapons. He would like to have flattened that hotshot forward. He was still ticked off at the way the guy had made Aiden look weak when he'd checked him into the boards.

As Aiden watched, a city transit bus pulled up and the defenceman climbed aboard, waving goodbye to the Walberg wimp as he heaved his equipment bag ahead of him onto the crowded bus.

Grabbing his own hockey bag, Aiden started over to where the forward stood waiting for his bus inside the shelter. He strode in, kicking Walberg's gear out of the way, and dropped his bag.

"What do you think you're doing, Walsh?" the kid asked.

Glancing at the forward, Aiden thought it was cool the guy knew his name. His reputation as an enforcer must be really getting around. Aiden was tall and quite husky for thirteen and this kid was a lot smaller and younger. "That's where I always put my bag." He sat on the bench. "You got a problem with that, *Walberg 33*?" He was aware of a heat beginning to build in him.

The slim boy started to say something, then looked around at the empty blackness of the street and just shrugged instead.

"You Rangers make good targets for a number-one team like the Devils." Aiden plopped his feet down on Walberg's hockey bag.

The Ranger forward gave him a look that seemed to be a direct challenge to Aiden. Aiden kicked the hockey bag with one of his boots. "Yeah, *Walberg 33*." He said the boy's name like it tasted bad in his mouth. "You guys are real wimps on the ice *and off*." He gave the Ranger player a sneer.

The young boy looked nervous as he reached for his bag. Aiden knocked his hand away with the toe of his boot. "I don't think so, *Walberg 33*."

"Get lost, you creep," the young forward said, but his voice had the telltale quaver in it Aiden had grown to know. The guy was shaking.

Aiden got up and stood on Walberg's equipment bag. "You want this, wimp? Come and get it." Aiden could feel the blood rushing to his face and his breath came in short bursts. Anger flooded him in a red rage.

The kid reached for the equipment bag and all of a sudden, Aiden felt like he was on fire. He jumped down off the bag and shoved the boy hard. The Ranger player fell back against the side of the bus shelter. Aiden's fist came out and hit the guy square in the face. He felt the boy's nose collapse under his blow.

Blood sprayed across the kid's face and covered Aiden's hand. The boy began yelling for help. "Shut up, you rotten loser!" Aiden shouted as he punched the now moaning boy again. The forward fell to the ground holding his bloodied nose.

Aiden was just going to start kicking the kid, when he felt his coat grabbed from behind, and he was nearly jerked off his feet.

"What the hell do you think you're doing?" It was Mr. Nichol, the Rangers' coach and he was furious. He looked huge as he loomed over Aiden.

"This wimp asked for it. He lipped off and I shut him up." Aiden tried to wrench his coat collar free, but the big man held onto it firmly.

"You punk, Walsh! You picked on the wrong kid this time. I've heard about you from other coaches and it's going to be my pleasure to take this game to a whole new level!" The burly man helped the bloodied forward to his feet and together all three of them headed back into the arena.

Aiden couldn't believe what happened after that.

His dad had come into the building looking for him just as Coach Nichol finished calling the wimp Walberg's parents. Aiden's dad had moved to Canada from Scotland and still spoke with a thick Glasgow accent. He was big and muscular with no hair on his head, which went red when he was angry. It was bright red now. He stormed around, yelling and waving his arms, as the coach called the police.

Aiden sat at a table in the corner of the room, feeling very uncomfortable as he watched Charlie build up a head of steam. He knew what that meant; somebody was going to get *straightened out*, which was how his dad put it just before he hit you.

Aiden rubbed his neck in a gesture he always did when he was feeling less than wonderful. He had a birthmark there, which he was very self-conscious about. His dad said it showed Aiden was physically weak, like his mom who also had a birthmark on her neck. But where Aiden's was big and dark-coloured, hers was small and shaped like a little pink heart. Aiden had always liked his mom's special mark.

She didn't live with them anymore, from the time his parents had gotten divorced. When she found out about tonight, she was not going to be happy. She never yelled or hit him when she was upset and somehow, that was even worse than if she'd smacked him. He could handle that. It was the disappointment in her face that really chewed him to pieces.

Aiden looked up as two burly police constables arrived. He swallowed hard. Although he'd had several run-ins at school for fighting that had ended up at the counsellor's office and he'd been in trouble for excessive force on the ice, he'd never been involved with the police before.

"Don't worry, boy," Charlie said, giving him a punch on the shoulder as he eyed the two constables. "This is just a lot of garbage. I'll have it all fixed in about two minutes flat." He nodded confidently, which made Aiden feel better.

But just then, the wimp's parents arrived. Coach Nichol urged Mr. and Mrs. Walberg, *Garth's* parents, to have Aiden charged with assault.

Aiden looked over at the Ranger forward. *Garth*, yeah, that suited the wimp. He hated that kid. His parents were going to take him to the hospital and see if his nose was broken, oh and yes, they would like Aiden charged.

Just like that! Aiden looked at the two policemen and then at the Ranger coach. If he had stayed out of this, everything would have been okay.

Coach Nichol nodded at Aiden. "You've been heading for this for a long time, Aiden. I just hope you can get yourself straightened out."

Straightened out! How Aiden hated those words. Furious, he glared back at the coach. "If the wimp could have looked after himself instead of needing a big jerk like you to butt in, none of this would be happening. It's not my fault the guy's such a spineless jellyfish." He was shouting and everyone was staring.

The two police officers nodded at one another as though everything had just been made very clear. One of them began writing up what Aiden thought would be something like a traffic ticket. His dad would simply pay it and that would be it.

"Sounds like you've got an attitude problem, son," the other constable said, frowning as he spoke. "Ordinarily, we'd have sent this directly to Alternative Measures, but in this case..." He shook his head and handed Charlie a piece of paper. "This is an Appearance notice, Mr. Walsh. You can take Aiden home with you, but what this paper means is that he will have to appear before a judge to have this matter heard."

Aiden nearly fell over. His legs suddenly felt like all the bones had been sucked out, but he knew Garth was watching him and there was no way he was going to look like a chicken in front of him. "That's garbage! The wimp had it coming!" He hoped he sounded tough.

Charlie looked at the document, his face twisted in rage, then stuffed it into his jacket pocket. "We'll see about this. Come on, boy," he growled as he turned to leave. "We'll straighten this out at home."

Aiden swallowed the lump in his throat and followed Charlie out of the arena. The temperature had dropped and the wind was now blowing straight out of the north. Slivers of icy sleet stung Aiden's cheeks and made his eyes water as he trudged after his dad.

2

Major Penalty

Waiting to go to court was a nightmare. Charlie was angry at first, and Aiden still remembered the sting of his dad's hand. But then they'd gone to the arcade. At the arcade, his dad's mood had lightened up and they'd had a great time. When he was in a good mood, Charlie wasn't cheap and they'd spent a lot of money on games and food.

Aiden had also spent extra time on his weightlifting. He hoped by lifting weights he would build his body up to look like the guys in the muscle magazines he liked to read. He couldn't lift very much now, but he knew if he kept at it, he would one day be as strong as Mr. Universe.

On Wednesday evening, before he was to go to court, Aiden was in the kitchen finishing the supper dishes when the phone rang. Charlie answered, then as he listened, his face became angry. "Look, Amy, the boy's doing fine. I'm telling you, it wasn't Aiden's fault. The other kid egged him on."

Aiden put the last dish away in the cupboard. It was his mom and he really wanted to talk to her. He would see her on Sunday, but that was a long time to wait. He and his mom usually spoke Tuesday and Thursday nights using their computers that had Internet web cameras and microphones so they could see and hear each other as they talked. The computer camera was really cool because Aiden didn't feel so alone when he could see her as they talked.

Sometimes when she phoned, Charlie would answer and get ticked off, then hang up before he had a chance to speak to her. That was why talking on his computer at night in his room was great. They could really talk without worrying Charlie was listening in and getting angry about something they said. This time, his dad just slammed the receiver on the counter. "It's your mother," he said, grabbing the paper and his coffee before heading to the living room.

Aiden seized the receiver, hoping his mom hadn't hung up. "Mom, I was hoping you'd call," he began. When his mom had left because she couldn't stay with Charlie anymore, Aiden had been so angry, he'd screamed that he hated her and the divorce was all her fault. He'd said he never wanted to see her again and he was staying with his dad.

He was sorry he'd said all that junk now. He and his mom had talked things over and everything was okay. It would have been better than okay if she'd come back, but Aiden knew that would never happen. He had to settle for their conversations on Tuesday and Thursday nights and his weekend visit on Sundays.

"I just called to tell you I'll be there tomorrow and not to worry. I'll help you get through this, whatever happens." Her voice was soft and soothing. "And Aiden, I love you, never forget that."

Aiden felt a lump in his throat. He swallowed hard. "I'm not worried, Mom. Charlie says we'll show them Walsh men ain't whiners and they can all go to h…."

"Aiden! Watch your language!" She paused and Aiden thought she was going to lecture him on using what she called *curse words*. "You'll show them Walsh men *aren't* whiners," she laughed and Aiden smiled. She was great! "Have you asked your dad about a dog yet?" she asked.

Aiden had always wanted a dog, but Charlie wouldn't hear of it. He said he had enough mouths to feed. Even when Aiden had signed up for his paper route to pay for the dog himself, his dad had said no. He'd been waiting for just the right moment to approach him again, but he didn't think now was a good time, not with the court stuff hanging over his head. "No, I think I'll wait till I have more money saved up first. Maybe after Christmas." His mom must have figured out what he was really trying to say, because she changed the subject.

They talked for a long time about why Aiden had beaten the boy up and he realized he didn't really know the answer. "Okay, Mom," he agreed. "If I had it to do over, I probably wouldn't smack the loser so hard."

"Aiden…" his mom's voice made him stop.

"Or maybe at all…" he finished guiltily.

"Better," she said with a sigh. They talked for a long time and when Aiden finally hung up, he felt relieved.

*   *   *

The day of his court appearance was just a blur to Aiden. All he remembered was the judge looking at him and frowning just before he had pronounced his sentence. "You, Mr. Walsh, are a lucky boy. We've got something a little different in mind for you. Three months' probation and one hundred hours' community service. That should keep you busy until nearly Christmas, young man. You will report to Mr. Michael Long Feather, your probation officer, every Saturday and *any further problems, such as the one that landed you here, will cause me to rethink how lenient I've been.*" He had looked at Aiden over the top of his small glasses, then had banged his gavel down.

Charlie had jumped up and yelled that Aiden had done nothing wrong and that the wimp had it coming. The yelling didn't help; Aiden still had to do the community service. His mom had hugged him and there were tears in her eyes. That had made him feel worse than anything the judge had said.

The next Saturday morning Aiden and his dad drove to the building where they would meet Mr. Michael Long Feather. It was an old sandstone structure with polished marble floors and the heels of Charlie's seldom-worn dress shoes clicked as he walked down the long corridor.

On a bench beside the probation officer's door, a strange-looking kid in crazy orange and green sunglasses sat with his parents. Aiden wondered what the skinny little runt had done to land his sorry butt here.

Once they were in Mr. Long Feather's office, Charlie began talking loudly. "This is just a crock. My boy shouldn't even be here. If that judge had been doing his job, those trumped-up charges against him would have been tossed."

Aiden thought Michael Long Feather wasn't very tough-looking at all. He was slight of build and about six inches shorter than Aiden's dad.

The probation officer sat quietly and let Charlie rant on, then he looked at Aiden. "Hi Aiden, I'm Michael Long Feather." His voice was quiet. "I know this must be pretty scary for you, but we *all* want to help. I've come up with a special community service that you might like — if you have the *right attitude*."

He looked at Aiden like he was waiting for him to swallow a dose of bad-tasting medicine. Aiden stared angrily right back. He wasn't the one with the attitude problem. This whole community service thing stunk. "Hey, are you some kind of

Indian?" he asked rudely.

The soft-spoken man stopped and then smiled like he didn't get the shot that Aiden had just given him. "Some kind. I'm a Mohawk from eastern Canada. My people are famous for working on high steel construction." He shrugged his shoulders. "But me, I'm a little nervous of heights, so I became a probation officer instead. I'm still not sure which job has more death-defying acts and heart-stopping action." He went on casually, "For your community service, you're going to be part of a new program. You get to be a companion for a young boy who would like a buddy on Saturdays. Your job is simple. You'll help him out when he needs it. And Aiden," he said, laying his pen on the table and looking hard at him, "*there will be absolutely no repetition of the bullying in any way, shape or form.* Is that clear?"

Aiden waited to hear what the rest of his punishment would be. When Michael stood up, ending the interview, Aiden couldn't believe his luck. This would be a cinch. He could put up with some whiney kid for a few weekends, then all this would be behind him and he could continue with his life.

"When does this whole thing start?" Charlie asked.

"Right now," Michael said, walking to the door.

Aiden and Charlie followed. They began walking over to the bench where the runt was sitting with his parents.

The three stood up and Aiden grinned to himself. This kid would be no problem. Besides being a runt, he was dressed like some nutcase from outer space. He had on a bright blue Hawaiian shirt with luminous yellow cargo pants twice as wide in the leg as any Aiden had seen and his wallet was fastened to his belt with a chain made of large multicoloured links. "You've got to be kidding!" Aiden muttered as he saw the Canada flag design on the kid's boxer shorts, which were sticking out of the top of his jeans.

"Aiden Walsh, I'd like you to meet Eric McLean," Michael said.

"Yeah, right." Aiden didn't try to hide the fact he found all of this a huge joke. He looked at Eric but couldn't see past the totally reflective lenses on his crazily coloured sunglasses.

"Great!" the runt said enthusiastically. "I've heard all about you, Aiden. I know we're going to have a blast." He grinned, showing a sizeable gap between his two front teeth, with the left tooth bigger than the right. Eric held out his hand to shake.

This guy was a real freak. Aiden looked at the outstretched hand, then grinned maliciously. "Oh, I bet we're going to have *a swell time*." He reached out and shook Eric's hand, squeezing with all his might. The kid might as well figure out how it's going to be right from the beginning.

Eric's smile never wavered. "Strong man, huh," he said, nodding.

"The adults can leave now," Michael said, dismissing the parents. "I'll be with the boys today, just to make sure everyone understands the rules." He gave Aiden a meaningful look.

Charlie snorted in disgust. "I'll be down at the pub with my buddies. Meet you at home later, boy." He turned and left, his broad shoulders hunching slightly forward when he walked.

Eric's parents, looking as though they were about to sacrifice their son to some volcano god, followed.

Aiden took a deep breath and prepared to start his community service. Yeah, *babysitting service*, he laughed to himself.

Eric walked back over to get his coat. He bumped into the bench and his jacket slid off the seat and into the puddle his melting boots had made as he'd waited. He picked up the coat and, without even looking at the slushy stain, shrugged into his jacket. "Ready, steady, go troops!" he said cheerfully, reaching into his coat pocket and taking something out that looked like a folded up white stick. With a couple of quick movements, Eric unfolded the stick, locking the segments until he had a long white cane. He held the cane out in front of him and swept it back and forth as he moved toward Aiden.

"All set?" Michael asked as he returned from getting his own coat.

"You're blind!" Aiden choked, ignoring Michael and staring at the cane.

"Obviously, you're not," Eric said. "Which is good because one of us has to drive the getaway car." He laughed hysterically at his lame joke. "Just kidding, Michael!"

Aiden felt a little panicky. He'd never known a blind kid before. How could he do community service with a blind kid? He wasn't sure the freak should even be allowed out without his parents. He was real sure the weirdo shouldn't be with a normal guy like himself. He didn't know what to do. "What am I supposed to do with this loser?" he asked, turning to Michael.

"Whatever Eric says," Michael answered, patting Eric on his short dark hair. "He's the boss."

"I like the sound of that!" Eric said, chuckling as he headed for the door.

3

Freaks and Geeks

Eric decided they were going to the William Castell Public Library, which was only a few blocks from Michael's downtown office. Aiden watched, fascinated, as Eric navigated the busy sidewalk. His cane never stopped moving and he seemed to be able to avoid most of the people and obstacles. Once he walked into a bus bench by accident, apologized, and kept on going.

They were stopped at a street corner across from the library and Aiden noticed Eric seemed to be listening for something. Aiden couldn't hear anything but the usual noises of traffic and pedestrians hurrying across the intersection.

Suddenly, Eric headed off across the street at the precise second the crossing signal turned to "walk." Aiden frowned, and followed. How had he done that? He couldn't possibly have seen the signal.

They entered the sliding door of the tall library building. "I'll wait here in the coffee shop, while you two get the books," Michael said, turning into the café on the ground floor of the big building.

"Hey, will you check if they have any of those Ooey-gooey Very-cherry Chocolate Squares? This is the only place that makes anything that cool." Eric took out his wallet and pulled out a five-dollar bill. "Take this five, my man. Ooey-gooeys for all my friends."

Aiden wondered how he knew the bill was a five. He surreptitiously eyed Eric's wallet and noticed it was arranged strangely. He had coins in the front pocket, carefully folded five-dollar bills on one side and a couple of differently folded tens on the other half of the billfold compartment.

"I'll take care of it," Michael said, waving away the money. "You two have fun."

Aiden watched as Eric refolded the five and carefully stashed it in his wallet. "Hey, Runt," he asked curiously. "How do you know what you're handing out and how come you have so much money on you?"

Ignoring his new nickname, Eric stuffed the wallet back in his baggy jeans. "I can feel the coins; twoonies are a different shape than loonies. The ten and five-dollar bills have raised dots on them that I can feel, but I also fold the tens in a special way so I don't mistake them for fives, which I just fold in half. That's how I tell the two bills apart and since I'm rarely lucky enough to have a twenty, there's no problem. Simple. I have a very tidy wallet. Everything has a place and a place for everything. And as for carrying such a big bankroll, it's my mom. She worries I'll get lost; my battery will go dead and I'll need to get a cab. She says it's better to be safe than sorry." Eric headed over to the elevators.

"What battery?" Aiden asked, hurrying to stay up with Eric, who moved with surprising speed.

Eric reached into his pocket and extracted a tiny cell phone. He waggled the small device in Aiden's general direction. "My mom's not really high-tech. She thinks the phone is tricky to operate and has no faith in rechargeable batteries or my ability to keep them charged." The elevator doors opened and Eric walked in. He slid his fingers down the side of the panel until he came to the fifth-floor button.

Again Aiden wondered how he did it. "How did you…" he began, feeling like an idiot.

"Braille numbers," Eric answered before Aiden could finish his question.

It was then that Aiden noticed the small raised dots beside each of the elevator buttons. "Oh, yeah. I just never noticed before," he said defensively.

"That's because you didn't need to. No worries! You're brand new to the world of the visually challenged and I've had thirteen years to learn all the tricks." Aiden felt like he'd been let off some kind of *idiot hook*. Eric went on speaking. "I love elevators that are set up like this. It really bites when the elevator panel is a blank piece of metal, because then you have to get someone to help you. One day I spent twenty minutes riding a stupid elevator because I lost count of the dumb floors and couldn't find the one I wanted." He held up his hand before Aiden could comment. "Shh, here comes my girlfriend."

Aiden was confused, and then a recorded woman's voice announced *second floor: children's books, Young Adult Theatre, John Dutton Theatre.*

"Man, that's a voice to dream over." Eric whistled through his two front teeth in admiration.

Aiden shook his head thinking this guy was a real freak. He wondered why they weren't going to the floor with young adult books.

The elevator stopped again and the recording said *fifth floor, special needs services*. As the door opened, Eric blew a kiss in the general direction of the speaker and marched off the elevator. "So long, sweetheart."

Aiden followed. The room was filled with shelves containing what looked like hundreds of videocassette boxes.

"Here's where you start earning your pay, old buddy. I need you to go get these books for me, please." He held out a list of titles.

"What am I supposed to do with this?" Aiden asked, grabbing the paper. There were no books on the shelves.

"This floor is only for the visually impaired," Eric explained. "These are book tapes. Ordinary books are recorded onto cassettes or CDs so kids like me can listen to them. It's how I stay so current with the hottest best-sellers."

Aiden looked at the list. There were familiar titles such as *Hockey: a History of the Game*, *Behind the Goalie's Mask* and *Goal-Scoring Secrets*. "What are you going to do with these? Hockey's got to be out of your league, Runt."

Again, Eric didn't rise to Aiden's bait. Instead, he began humming a pop tune and tapping out a beat with his cane.

Frustrated at being ignored, but knowing he couldn't lay a finger on the runt, Aiden stomped off and began looking for the titles.

After checking out the book tapes, they met Michael back in the lobby.

"Did you get our Ooey-gooeys?" Eric asked hopefully.

"Yes," Michael said, touching Eric on the arm to let him know where the small brown paper bag was. "But I think we should go for burgers before you dive into this."

"Okay, but be warned. The noise from my stomach growling will force us to turn up the radio real loud for the drive there." Eric took the bag and stashed it in one of his roomy pockets.

*   *   *

"You guys head in. I've got a couple of calls to make, then I'll join you," Michael said, pulling into the parking lot of a Burger Barn.

Aiden was glad he'd brought money so that he was able to turn Michael down when he offered to buy. He didn't want to owe Michael Long Feather anything, not after what the jerk had done to him — saddling him with a geek like this obnoxious runt.

They stood in line for a long time and Aiden began losing patience. When the boy in front of them couldn't make up his mind, Aiden shook his head in disgust. "We don't have all day. Back of the line!" he snarled and shoved the kid out of his way. The boy started to protest, but Aiden ignored him.

"Nothing for me," Eric said adjusting his gaudy sunglasses.

"Suit yourself, Runt. I'm starving." Aiden ordered his food. The boy he'd shoved glared at him, but didn't say anything.

The order was ready quickly and as Aiden got his money out, Eric reached past him and took the tray with the great-smelling burger and fries.

Aiden finished paying and turned just in time to see Eric handing the tray to the boy he'd shoved.

"Sorry about my friend," Eric said, grinning at the boy. "He gets a little cranky when he hasn't had his nap." The boy smiled and took the food-laden tray, then quickly moved to a table as far away from Aiden as he could get.

Aiden became instantly furious. He was just about to teach Eric a lesson, when Michael walked in.

"Have you boys ordered yet?" Michael asked, walking up to them.

"Nope," Eric said, moving to the counter. "We thought we'd wait for you. Right, Aiden? Man, I'm starving! Bring on the burgers!"

Aiden was so angry, he couldn't say anything. This babysitting thing wasn't working out like he'd thought it would.

4

Back in the Game

It was a long week, but finally Thursday night rolled around and with it, a game. He'd miss talking with his mom, but she understood how important hockey was to him.

The Devils were playing the Kensington Dragons and they were stoked. Aiden relaxed as his skates hit the polished surface of the ice. He felt powerful as he did his warm-up. Whenever he thought about the crummy incident he'd had at the burger joint with that runt Eric McLean, it put him in the mood for some payback. He wasn't going to allow a repeat performance on Saturday.

As the teams finished their warm-up, Aiden skated past the Dragons' net and blasted a hard slapshot at the goalie. The surprised netminder wasn't expecting the shot and the puck sailed past his head and into the top shelf. Grinning as the goalie cursed, Aiden headed for the Devils' bench.

"You up to protecting our new star player?" Coach Goldstein asked Aiden as he came off the ice.

Aiden looked around. He didn't see any new players. "Yeah, sure. Who's the new guy?" he asked.

"Not a new guy. It's Jamie Cook. He's really shone lately and his last game was great! I want you to cover him so he can concentrate on scoring." Just then, Jamie came off the ice and the coach slapped him on the back. "You're going to be the highest scorer in the league, right, Jamie?"

Jamie grinned at him through his wire face mask. "Right, Coach!"

Aiden looked at Jamie, instantly angry. When had Cook turned into a hotshot? Jamie had been good at setting up plays and assists, but Aiden was always too busy crushing guys to notice how many goals he scored.

Aiden had never told anyone, especially Charlie, who thought being an enforcer was the best thing in hockey, but he'd always secretly wanted to be a high-scoring hero who got all the cheers. Most people treated him like the guy who killed cows in a meat packing plant — a necessary evil, but not someone you wanted to bring home for Sunday dinner.

When the whistle blew, Aiden went into action. He started by chopping the defenceman he was covering behind the shin pads. In the jostling for the puck, the refs never saw that one, but the defenceman nearly went down. It let one of Aiden's teammates, Jesse Esposito, scoop the puck and turn toward the Dragons' end.

Aiden felt great. He looked for another target. The Dragons were a tight team and knew how to play defensive hockey. They were good at intercepting the play at the blue line and trying for a breakout.

Although he never got to use his other skills very much, Aiden was sure he was a match for any player on the ice. He was always practising his drills and could pick off a pass better than anyone — including his ex-buddy Jamie Cook. The thought of Jamie being the star player for the Devils bugged Aiden. And as for goal-scoring technique, he knew he was a better sniper than the know-it-all captain any day of the week.

Aiden zeroed in on a Dragon player who was skating too

close to the Devils' net. He came in fast, knocking the boy backward off his skates. The kid went down hard and slid into the boards as Aiden skated past. Unfortunately, as Aiden blasted around the far corner of the net, he almost collided with Tyler Hart, one of his own teammates. He shouldered the Devil forward out of the way and started back toward centre ice.

Up near the blue line, Aiden spotted Jamie dicing with two Dragon players. Putting on a burst of speed, Aiden moved in between Jamie and the two offensive players. A quick elbow to the chest finished off one and a fast hook with his stick took care of the other. Just as Jamie scooped the puck and broke for the net, the ref's whistle stopped the play.

Aiden saw the ref pointing at him and making a tugging motion with both arms, as though he were pulling something toward him. "Oakridge Devils, number thirteen, two minutes, hooking!" the ref called.

Aiden turned for the penalty box, grinning. The ref had missed the elbowing completely. He settled in the penalty box and glanced at the stands. Charlie waved and tapped his elbow with his hand, the signal for elbowing, then gave Aiden the thumbs-up.

His dad was cool. He could spot dirt that refs never even suspected. Aiden tried to be patient as he put in his time. He frowned, watching the Dragon goalie. There was something wrong about the way the guy was standing. Then he knew. The goalie, who used a butterfly style of netminding, was putting all his weight on the front of his skates and leaning too far forward. He'd be off balance and easy to get one past if the shooter used a low fake, then fired one up top.

Aiden knew he could do it easily. He suddenly wanted out of the penalty box. The second the timekeeper released him, Aiden began streaking toward the Dragons' end. Jamie and

Jesse had possession of the puck and were working it down ice toward the Dragon end, but way too slowly. The goalie would have time to correct his poor stance and they'd never beat him.

Aiden moved up beside Jamie. "Pass me the puck. I know how to get it past their goalie!" he shouted.

"I'm taking this one in, Aiden. Give me some protection!" Jamie yelled back.

Aiden didn't want to give him any protection. He wanted to score a goal. "I said *give me the puck!*" he yelled, lifting Jamie's stick and stealing the puck for himself. Aiden could hear Jamie swearing as he turned for his run at the goal.

The goalie was still standing wrong and when he went for Aiden's low fake shot, he overbalanced and fell to his knees. Before he could spring back up, Aiden fired a sizzler, top right corner. The goal light whirled!

Aiden punched the air and shook his stick. Winner! Satisfied he'd done a great job, he headed for the bench.

"What do you think you're doing, Walsh?" Coach Goldstein asked the second Aiden came through the gate. "Your job is to cover the shooters, which means running tough interference for Jamie, not stripping the puck and going for the glory yourself. On this team, players follow team orders."

Aiden stopped, confused. He should have been getting congratulations, not this. The happiness he'd just felt evaporated into the chilly air.

The coach laid a hand on Aiden's shoulder. "Look, Aiden, we both know you shine as a guy who can keep order on the ice. You're great at your job, but I want you to stick to taking troublemakers out. Okay?" He smiled at Aiden, who just nodded glumly back.

For the rest of the game, Aiden concentrated on taking Dragon players out. He didn't think what the coach said was fair. He'd proven he could score with the best of them. He'd called the play exactly.

The Devils won 9-3, which made Aiden feel a little better. He was sitting on the bench in the dressing room, when Jamie Cook and Tyler Hart approached him. They didn't look happy. He unconsciously rubbed his neck, covering the birthmark as he did so. "What's biting your butts?" Aiden asked, looking at his two teammates.

"You are, Aiden. I don't know what's going on with you lately, but you've changed," Jamie began, his voice tight with anger. "What did you think you were doing out there tonight?"

"My job!" Aiden narrowed his eyes. "Do you have a problem with that, Cook?"

"You stole a scoring opportunity from me. I could have taken that Dragon goalie and you know it." Jamie's voice was loud and everyone was staring.

Aiden felt his hands curling into fists.

"And you nearly put me into the goalpost when you shouldered me out of the way," Tyler complained.

Aiden vaguely remembered bumping into Tyler when he'd taken out that kid who ended up kissing the boards. He'd hardly noticed the hit. "Look, I don't play wimp-style hockey. It was made very clear to me that my job is muscle, so that's what I do." He grabbed his equipment bag.

"We're supposed to play as a team, Aiden," Jamie said, his voice more reasonable now. "I thought we were friends and friends are supposed to help each other."

"Yeah, well, I *helped* myself to a goal," Aiden said, hoisting the big bag over his shoulder. "Because you sure wouldn't have given me a chance to score, would you, Cook?" He strode out, his stomach twisted in a knot of anger.

When he walked into the arena concourse, his mom was

standing with Charlie. Aiden was surprised to see her, but immediately felt better. She was shaking her head, making her shoulder-length blonde hair swirl around her face. She was small and delicate, but looked really tiny standing next to Charlie's hulking form.

"Hi, Mom, what are you doing here? Did you see me get that sweet goal?" Aiden asked, grinning.

"I thought that since it was Thursday and we wouldn't get a chance to visit on the computer, I'd put in a personal appearance. And as for the goal, I certainly did!" his mom said, hugging him. Aiden smelled the perfume that he'd given her for her birthday. It made him feel good to think she still liked it enough to continue wearing the flowery scent. "I think you should be given the chance to score more goals. You made it look awfully darn easy." She smiled at him. "Maybe you should talk to your coach about being a goal scorer — "

"Wrong!" Charlie cut in, loudly. "What do you know about hockey? You only got interested in the game when Aiden started playing. My boy here is the best darn enforcer in the league," he said proudly. "He can pick off guys like a sharpshooter at a county fair."

Aiden smiled at his dad, then brushed his still sweat-damp hair back off his forehead. It was getting so long the gel he used wouldn't keep his spikes upright. The tips were a cool white and having his hair cut would mean he'd have to bleach them out again. Usually he'd have his hair cut on a Saturday, but he couldn't now that he had to hang out with the weirdo Eric McLean.

"Amy, you know nothing about what it takes to play this game," his dad said, rounding on his mom. "Just try and stay out of it, for once."

His voice had that edge to it that Aiden and his mom knew well.

His mom's voice had a slight quaver in it when she spoke. "I'm not going to argue with you, Charlie. Those days are over." She turned to her son. "I'd better go now, Aiden. It was a wonderful game, honey." She looked into his eyes. "Remember, you can call me anytime, day or night." She smiled at him, then walked away.

Aiden silently watched her go.

"Great game, boy!" Charlie said, interrupting Aiden's thoughts as he enthusiastically clapped his son on the back. "You sucked that goalie right out of his skates!" He was grinning. "Man, you were really something," he added, punching his son on the arm.

Aiden ignored the light hit. "Yeah, I remembered everything you taught me back when we used to practise together, you know the stuff about looking for a weakness, then using it to your advantage." He smiled. "Man, that was a sweet goal, wasn't it! I'm glad Mom was here to see it." He gave his dad a sidelong glance. "I wouldn't mind being a hot shooter and getting some of the glory."

"And waste the way you keep order on the ice?" Charlie shook his head. "I think you should stick to your strengths, hone those skills. That's what those NHL scouts are going to be looking for."

Aiden didn't look at his dad. He liked what his mom had said. The idea of being a goal scorer was cool. But being an enforcer was important, too.

"That hotshot stuff's not for you, Aiden," Charlie went on. "Besides, there's a lot of times even super shooters can't score without the tough guys out there covering their butts and opening up opportunities for them. You really are good at your job, boy." His voice had softened and it made Aiden feel a little embarrassed to hear his dad talk like that.

"Right," Aiden agreed. "I'm the toughest Devil out there and if any of those second raters in the league don't remember that, I'll give them a little reminder." He said the words, knowing it was what Charlie expected.

5

Seeing Ice Dogs

Saturday morning Aiden finished his paper route early and sat glumly at the kitchen table eating his breakfast. He thought about Thursday's game and how he and Jamie had ended up fighting. It made him feel crummy. They used to get along great. They would talk about everything, not just hockey, and he had even stayed over at Jamie's house a couple of times. Aiden never invited anyone to stay at his house. Charlie didn't like other kids hanging around. Jamie had said he had changed. Aiden didn't think he had, except to get even tougher on the ice, but that was his job. Everyone said so.

Aiden wasn't looking forward to his day with Eric McLean. Not only was it a total waste of his Saturday, but he had to listen to the runt's stupid jokes. The judge hadn't told him about that part. The only thing that would make this day bearable was that he had a Devils' game later and would get a chance to bounce some losers off the boards.

Michael picked him up promptly at nine o'clock. Because time would be tight, Michael would drop Aiden off at the arena for his game. He'd brought Aiden a steaming cup of hot chocolate, which he handed to him as soon as they were in the car and had their seat belts on. This surprised Aiden, especially when he never said a word about not spilling any on the upholstery like

Charlie would have.

"How's it going today, Aiden?" Michael asked.

"Okay, I guess," Aiden mumbled, shrugging his shoulders. He took a sip of the chocolate. He was still thinking about Jamie.

Michael glanced over at him. "Sounds like something's *not* so okay. Problems?" he prompted. "I know what that's like. Sometimes you feel like you're drowning in a bucket of slime and no one understands just how badly your world sucks. I found that sometimes just talking about it helps a lot." He stared straight ahead at the road.

Aiden was a little surprised Michael used words like *slime* and *sucks*. It made him seem so… normal. Still, telling Michael about his run-in with his teammates was out of the question. What business was it of his anyway?

He decided to tell Michael to butt out, but when he opened his mouth, that's not what happened. "I'm really ticked off about my teammate and ex-friend Jamie Cook," he blurted out. "We used to be buddies, but not anymore and that's another thing that stinks." He thought about the good times he'd had with Jamie and how they used to talk about everything. "I really liked Jamie, but not now!" he exploded.

Michael glanced over at him again. "Go on," was all he said.

Aiden did go on, surprised at his own anger. "The coach has him slated to be the number-one goal scorer, and it's just not fair. Has the coach ever asked me if I wanted to try scoring more goals instead of nuking kids left, right and centre? No way! He just figures I like pounding on kids." He was on a roll now and wasn't going to stop. It was as though he couldn't control what came out of his mouth.

Aiden took a deep breath and continued. "I can stickhandle

and score better than anyone on the team. Sure, I'm good at taking guys out and running interference, but I can play more hockey than that. I can play *great* hockey! I just never get the chance." He finished, stunned at his own outburst and more than a little embarrassed. He hadn't meant to say any of that stuff.

"Have you told the coach you want to be a goal scorer?" Michael asked.

"The coach knows where I play best," Aiden said lamely, then added, "I'm an enforcer, maybe the toughest guy in the league." He knew he should be proud of this because he was great at it, but right now, he didn't feel like bragging.

"But you still want to score goals, right? Are there rules that say you can't be tough *and* a high scorer?" Michael looked at him. "Maybe shoving guys around isn't what you really want to do all the time. You said Jamie was your *ex*-friend, why is that?"

Aiden thought about this. He remembered he and Jamie had been good friends before Charlie had told him he was acting like a wimp and had *straightened him out*. Aiden had become a lot tougher after that.

It had been right around the time Aiden had started putting those losers at school in their place and going for detention a lot more because of it. Jamie had said he didn't like having a friend who was always fighting and had stopped calling him. The memory came flooding back and for some reason it made Aiden feel uncomfortable and a little sad. "How am I supposed to know?" he said defensively. "Jamie Cook is a wimp, just like all the rest. Now, can we drop it?"

He looked out the window at the icy trees. They had a thick lacy coating of glittering frost and when Aiden stared, he could see diamonds winking back as the sun glinted off the branches. Neither of them spoke for the rest of the trip to Eric's house.

"Eric is in his room upstairs, first door on the right," Mrs. McLean said, smiling warmly as they stood in the entranceway of Eric's house. "Why don't you go up, Aiden."

"Good idea. I want to talk to Mr. and Mrs. McLean about some details. Give me about fifteen minutes, will you?" Michael asked.

Aiden nodded, wondering if the runt had squealed about the incident at the Burger Barn, but since Michael hadn't gone nuts on him, he didn't think so. They probably just wanted to talk about him behind his back.

Eric was sitting on his bed, pulling on his socks when Aiden walked into the room.

"Is my little buddy here, yet?" Eric asked, looking up. He had wild glow-in-the-dark green sunglasses on today. "Mom? Dad?" he asked, hesitantly.

Aiden felt strange, he didn't know what to say or how to talk to a blind guy. "It's me, Runt. I'm supposed to stay up here while your parents and Michael have a little chat. You didn't say anything I should know about, did you, because that wouldn't be so smart." His voice sounded ominous and he hoped this annoying punk got the message.

"Hey, I wouldn't spill the beans to my folks about anything a buddy and I did!" Eric grinned, showing his uneven front teeth. "That wouldn't be cool."

Aiden noticed Eric's getup was even weirder today. He had on black jeans with silver studs down the outside of the legs, which were even wider than the last pair. Added to this was a brilliant red T-shirt with a cartoon drawing of a kid skateboarding on it that had to be three sizes too big for him and to finish it off, the geek had socks on that didn't match.

"What's that girlie thing you've got around your neck?" Aiden asked, noticing the necklace Eric had on. It looked like it was made out of hundreds of small white discs all strung together.

"Isn't it great! My uncle brought it back from Hawaii for me. It's made of puka shells." Eric touched the necklace as though it were made out of rare jewels.

"*Puke-a* shells!" Aiden scoffed. "You're kidding me! What a loser."

Eric thought about this, then began laughing so hard his nose made a snorting sound. "*Puke-a*, good one. Disgustingly gross, but a good one."

Aiden looked around at the posters on Eric's walls, noticing with surprise that they were all hockey players. And not just current ones; he also had pictures of old stars like Rocket Richard, Eddy Shack and Bobby Orr. He had Gretzky, Jagr, Messier and Lemieux, Shanahan, Mogilny and Coffey. On the wall above his bed and circled with paper cut-outs of hockey pucks was a picture of Eric Lindros. Lindros was obviously the runt's hero.

"Why do you have all these posters? A guy like you doesn't need them, that's for sure. You may as well put up paper grocery bags," Aiden snickered. It was then that he noticed a lot of the posters were hand autographed with a personal message to Eric.

"Great!" Eric sighed theatrically, slapping his forehead. "Now you tell me! Do you know how much of my allowance money I have invested in these babies?" He shook his head. "I wish you'd told me this years ago."

Aiden couldn't believe this guy. Didn't he ever get ticked off? "Look, Runt, hockey is a real jock's game. You need to *play* to understand what goes on and that's something you'll never do." He hoped this time that he'd scored a hit on the obnoxious kid.

Eric felt his wristwatch, touching a button on the side. The watch spoke the time out loud! "Not for at least another hour, anyway." He nodded at Aiden. "Let me get my stuff together and we can go."

It was then that Aiden noticed the hockey equipment bag in the corner and a Koho stick leaning against the wall. He frowned, confused. "What are you getting at, Runt?" He walked over and looked in the bag. There were Bauer skates, Jofa pads, and a CCM helmet as well as a bright red jersey with a picture of a white dog holding a hockey stick in his mouth on the front. The stick was coloured the same way Eric's white cane had been, with the bottom end red, white in the middle and the remaining hand grip, black. Aiden couldn't believe what he saw printed on the back of the shirt. There, in big white letters was *McLean, 88.*

"You play hockey!" Aiden was flabbergasted. "That's impossible! No way! How? You can't see!"

"No kidding, Sherlock!" Eric said. "I not only play, but I rock!" He got up and went over to his bag. "Hockey and I were made for each other." He hefted his equipment bag onto his shoulder and grabbed his stick. "And you, Aiden, my man, get to see *The Great Eric* in action today. The *Calgary Seeing Ice Dogs*, that's the team I play for, have a practice today. We're the heroes. Let the good times roll!" He started downstairs whistling a tune between his teeth as he went.

Aiden didn't know what to say. How could a kid who couldn't see play hockey? This was not what he expected to do today, but he'd take hockey over babysitting any day.

*   *   *

The rink looked ordinary enough. The nets were regulation; the ice had the usual markings, and the players circling as they warmed up were as familiar to Aiden as his own team. There was one difference. These players were spread over a much wider age range. Eric seemed to be the youngest player suited up. Some of the other skaters were a lot older, but it didn't seem to matter. They were all playing together. Another thing Aiden noticed was that they had different-coloured helmets on. Some wore red, some black and a few had white ones.

Aiden sat in the players' box with Eric and watched the skaters.

"Okay, here's the scoop," Eric began. "Even though there are blind teams right across Canada, there's only one here in Calgary, so we take anyone who has talent or who is at least interested and the bonus part is, you don't have to be blind to play," he chuckled. "The players with the black helmets, like mine, are totally blind and that includes our goalies," he explained. "The guys with the red ones have less than 10 per cent vision and the skaters out there with the white helmets; they can see. Usually half the skaters on the ice can see. That way, if the puck stops moving, which means the visually impaired players don't know where it is, the sighted guys can dig it out of the corners and get it back in play. Once it's moving, we know where the puck is because our puck is a little different."

He handed Aiden a metal disc about ten centimetres across and six centimetres thick. "The flat sides curve out, making it tippy so when it's wiggling down ice we can hear it." He shook the puck and it rattled loudly. "There are metal ball bearings inside that make lots of noise, as long as the little devil is moving. That's how we know where it is. Oh, and you can't lift the puck off the ice because then the rattling stops and we're in trouble. It's pretty hard to stop a puck you can't hear. Only blind players can score, so they're usually forwards and sighted skaters are defencemen."

He turned to Aiden. "One important detail. We don't check players to take them out permanently. We use skill and judgement when we check a guy. It's a lot tougher to do than to just blow them off the ice. There aren't that many blind hockey players around, so we like to keep the ones we have healthy."

He nodded toward the ice. "Watch for a while. We're going to have a little game of shinny. The rules are about the same as any regulation game." He started clambering over the boards. "Prepare to be dazzled."

Michael walked up behind Aiden in the players' box and dropped a pair of skates behind the bench. "I think you'll enjoy watching these guys. They're really good."

Aiden scoffed as he watched the skaters warming up. "How could they be? They're blind."

Michael smiled wryly. "Maybe they try harder than the average player."

"They could try all they want, but it won't help them play hockey." Aiden slumped on the bench as Eric skated back to the box.

"Hey, Aiden, we're short a player for our shinny game. You want to fill in?" Eric waited for an answer.

Aiden snorted. "Me, play with you! I'm out of your league, Runt."

Michael reached behind the bench and lifted Aiden's skates up, holding them in the air. "I just happened to bring your blades along. Care to put your skates where your mouth is?" he asked.

Aiden glanced at Eric and thought about being able to legally crush this arrogant little wimp into the boards. He realized he'd been set up. Reaching for his skates, he shrugged his shoulders. "How tough could it be?" he said with a smirk.

6

Seeing Is Believing

Aiden's team, the *A Squad*, consisted of four guys and a goalie, which left them a man short. Eric, wearing a black helmet signalling he was totally blind, was a forward; Jeff Galbraith, the other forward, wore a red helmet, which meant he had less than 10 per cent sight. The goalie, Brian Clark, was blind and wore a black helmet.

The remaining player had on a white helmet and could see. "Hi, I'm Kevin Gardner and we play defence," he said, handing Aiden a white helmet. "Our forwards, Jeff and Eric, will be the only ones allowed to score. We need to help set them up and take out the bad guys."

"What do I do?" Aiden asked, confused as to how he was supposed to babysit these guys once the puck dropped.

"Play hockey!" Kevin said, moving to centre ice. "Since we're short a centre, you take this faceoff, Aiden," Kevin called.

Aiden followed with all the confidence that came from knowing he was good. The wannabes were in for a treat. He could skate circles around these chumps.

The noisy metal puck dropped and Aiden reached out to snag it from the *B Squad*'s centre, whose jersey said "Cameron" and his red helmet meant he was visually impaired. Aiden couldn't believe it when, with lightning speed, this Cameron guy stole the puck and turned for the net, his defenceman clos-ing in smoothly, cutting Aiden off from attack.

"Eric, on your left, going in for a shot!" Kevin called as he turned to follow the puck carrier.

"Come on, Aiden," Eric yelled. "Randy Cameron's got a wicked slapshot. We've got to take the *can* away from him or we're in trouble!"

Aiden took the rink in at a glance. Cutting left, he moved around the two skaters covering him and went after the puck carrier. He had to push to catch the attacking skater. This Cameron guy could really fly.

Just as Aiden caught up with him, the red-helmeted forward pulled his stick back and fired a bullet at their goalie, Brian Clark. No one could have stopped that shot. It flashed past Brian, who made a great grab at it, but the shooter was just too fast.

Aiden re-evaluated his opinion of the Seeing Ice Dogs. He decided no more Mr. Nice Guy and set out to show these guys how to play, but it didn't go that way. He was all set to receive a backhand pass from Eric, when one player from the opposing squad who had on a red helmet, cut in and scooped the puck right out from under Aiden's stick. He cursed and went after the skater whose jersey said his name was Rogalsky.

There was a lot more chatter on the ice than in a regular game and now, everyone cheered on the Rogalsky guy for scooping the new kid. Aiden felt himself growing angry. A cou-ple of plays later, Aiden stole the puck and headed for the goalie, Gary Zarbock, whose black helmet meant he was blind. Aiden came in hard and cut around the back of the net figuring on an easy wraparound, but when he fired, there was the goalie with his big blade ready. The puck deflected back out to a wait-ing defenceman who picked it up and passed it up ice to a guy with a red helmet who headed straight for the net. Aiden could feel his face burn as the other guys teased him.

"Just blind guys are allowed to score," Eric reminded him. "Or should I say *try* to score!" He skated off, laughing.

Aiden cursed to himself and headed back after the play. By the time the mock game had finished, the B Squad was two goals in the lead and Aiden was furious. He felt like an idiot as the other skaters slapped him on the back for a *great effort*.

Great effort! He was ready to smash something. Aiden stormed off the ice and practically tore his skates off. "Can we take this freak home now?" he demanded as Michael came into the players' box. "I've got a real game to play against real hockey players."

Michael looked at him and raised one eyebrow. "Sure, but we're going to take Eric home first."

On the ride home, Eric kept telling Michael about what a great job Aiden had done and how hard it was to get used to all the cross-rink chatter and the way Aiden was able to deke out the guys even though they'd been playing together for a long time and how no one had been able to stump them before.

Aiden could feel himself boiling as the runt blabbed on.

"This was a lot of fun," Eric said, not noticing Aiden's icy silence as they stopped in front of his house. "I can hardly wait to see what you do for an encore. I hope we didn't tire you out too much for your game tonight."

"As if, Runt. I never even broke a sweat." Aiden tried to sound casual. There was no way he was going to tell this punk how hard he'd really worked.

*   *   *

Unfortunately, Aiden's bad mood carried over to the Devils'

game that night.

"Man, Aiden, I think you've set a new record for penalty minutes in a game," Jamie said as he and Aiden headed to the dressing room after a dismal match. The Devils had lost by one point.

Aiden was instantly ready to fight. "Lay off, Cook. Half those penalties were bogus. I think the ref was out to get me." He tossed his stick into the corner. "I didn't lose the game. I did my job. You're supposed to be the hotshot scorer. Maybe you should have pulled down a couple more goals."

Jamie didn't say anything more; instead he just shook his head and started to change into his street clothes.

Aiden was still smoking mad when Charlie picked him up.

"What's eating you?" Charlie asked as Aiden threw his hockey bag into the back of the truck.

"Nothing," Aiden answered sullenly.

"Come on boy, you took some penalties, but that's part of the game." He paused. "It's not like you were pushed around on the ice or anything, but you seemed to be dragging tonight."

Aiden knew that Charlie was trying to be nice, but he was suddenly reminded of his humiliation that afternoon. "Okay, I screwed up. If I'd spent more time on the ice and less on penalties, maybe the Devils wouldn't have lost, but I was tired from this afternoon." He knew as soon as he'd said it that it was a mistake.

Charlie pounced on it like a cat on a mouse. "Why? What happened?"

He took a deep breath and explained about playing with the Seeing Ice Dogs. Charlie was at first skeptical, then outright angry.

"Let me get this straight. You let a bunch of handicapped skaters wipe up the ice with you? You were out-skated and out-stickhandled by a bunch of wimps?" He hit the steering wheel with his fist. "What's the matter with you, boy?"

Aiden's temper flared. "You should have seen those guys. I think the McLean punk set me up. Michael had my skates and practically made me play. He's my probation officer; I couldn't say no." He rubbed his neck where his birthmark was. He knew he was making up excuses that would only make Charlie angrier. He decided to steer things back to safer ground. "I screwed up tonight, but I'm still the toughest enforcer out there. Did you see the way I hit that stupid forward and sent him into the net on top of their goalie? I hit him so hard his lumber ended up across the blue line."

Charlie grinned, remembering the spectacular hit. "Yeah, that was what I like to see. My boy dominating the ice. That Cook kid wouldn't have made half the goals he got without you clearing the track for him."

Aiden was instantly boiling again. Jamie had pulled down a hat trick tonight and owed Aiden two of those goals. He had taken out the defence so Jamie had a clean run at the goalie. All the coach had said was to watch his penalty minutes. Nice.

*   *   *

The next week at school was a disaster. Aiden had forgotten to do a homework assignment and when his math teacher had called on him he had been unable to give her the answer to question four. He was angry with himself. He knew how to do the problems; he just didn't get around to finishing the work. The wimp who sat behind him had snickered and called him a stupid goon. Aiden's temper boiled over and he had thumped the creep after school, but been caught by his teacher. When she was unable to reach Charlie, she'd contacted Michael Long Feather.

Aiden sat in the counsellor's office, waiting.

"I thought we had an understanding," Michael said as soon as he walked through the door.

"Yeah. I'm supposed to leave that runt McLean alone. This has nothing to do with him," Aiden said defensively. He didn't look at Michael.

"I don't think you understand. You can't get into *any* trouble or you'll end up in front of the judge again. I'm supposed to write a report on your progress and if I include crud like this, you'll be washed out. That judge did you a favour, but he's not going to like hearing about your ongoing career as a thug." Michael took a deep breath. "I'm really busy right now and don't have time to do all the paperwork this would involve." He glanced over at Aiden to see if he was listening. "So I'm going to cut you some slack."

Aiden pretended to be real interested in a piece of gum that was stuck to the tile floor, kicking it with the toe of his sneaker.

"This is what's going to happen. You will apologize to this kid you punched, then I have a new game plan for the next time you have the urge to take your frustration out on some unsuspecting classmate or hockey player or even the neighbourhood cat." Michael ran his hand through his short black hair. He was really ticked. "I want you to promise that you'll tell me when you're going to beat someone up *before you do it*. Agreed?"

Aiden looked up, surprised. *Before* he beat anyone up! "No problem," he said quickly, nodding his head. Sweet! After all, Michael had not threatened him or forbidden him to beat a kid up, he just wanted to *talk* to him first and since he only saw the probation officer once a week, this should work out nicely. If Aiden happened to forget to tell Michael about a fight he was planning, it would be understandable. A week was a long time and it could slip a guy's mind.

Michael took a small cell phone out of his pocket and handed it to Aiden. "I'm on speed dial and I'm available *twenty four-seven*. Oh, and don't even think about losing the phone. I would have to go to Charlie to reimburse me and I don't think either of us want that." He took a deep breath and sighed. "Look, Aiden. I'm not doing this to punish you. A lot of people have gone out of their way to give you a break, but you are teetering right on the edge of permanent disaster with your bullying. We don't want that to happen. You're a good kid and we all want you to succeed, to win." He looked at Aiden, a small smile on his face. "*I* want you to win."

Aiden hadn't expected this twist. He stared at the tiny phone in his hand. There was no way he could get away from Michael now and they both knew it.

He looked at Michael but could see no tricks or lying in the probation officer's face. Maybe this guy was for real. Maybe he did want to help.

7

Off-Ice Excitement

For several weeks, Aiden and Eric continued to do things on Saturdays. It wasn't always exciting, like playing hockey. Sometimes, Aiden would read to Eric out of hockey magazines or tell him about an exciting play on television. They would also play cards with Eric's special deck, which had Braille numbers.

Aiden discovered there were a lot of things made especially for non-sighted people, such as a talking calculator and clock, a computer with a voice program and synthesizer and a Braille labeller. Eric had all these high-tech gadgets, but he used the labeller the most. He had the small labels on lots of things in his room, like favourite books and tapes, CDs and even pictures. Once they had gone swimming and Eric had walked into the ladies' changing room by accident, at least he'd said it was *by accident*, but he'd grinned all the way home.

Several times, Aiden had come close to getting in a fight, but Eric would always butt in and talk to him about the other guy's side. It was frustrating because by the time Eric finished yakking, either Aiden didn't feel much like fighting or the wimp had run away. When he told Michael about this, Michael would talk to him about why he wanted to fight in the first place and what had stopped him.

"Well, how do you like me so far?" Eric had asked him late one Saturday afternoon.

Aiden thought about this for a minute. The runt was smart and he never got angry or had to prove himself. He let a lot of stuff slide that Aiden would have had to pound someone for. "I guess you're not too obnoxious," he said, shrugging his shoulders. Then he added, "For a runt."

One Friday afternoon Aiden came home from school to an empty house. On the kitchen table was a message from Charlie. Michael had called to say he wouldn't be able to take him over to Eric's tomorrow and could Charlie drive instead.

His dad had added a line at the bottom. *I'm not doing any backflips for this Long Feather jerk. If he wants you to be with that wimp, then he can come and take you.*

Aiden sighed. Why did everything with Charlie have to be a fight? Crumpling the paper in his fist, he threw it in the garbage. He'd just take the bus.

Saturday morning, Aiden finished his paper route and headed out to the bus before Charlie was even out of bed. His dad had been out with his buddies the night before and had come in late. This was a stroke of luck for Aiden, as he didn't want to argue about taking the bus to Eric's.

When he arrived at the McLean house, Eric's mom had made brownies and insisted the boys have a snack before heading out.

"What lame thing do you want to do today?" Aiden asked, reaching for another of the delicious chocolate squares. Now that his mom wasn't living with them, he didn't get homemade treats very often.

Eric, looking as bizarre as ever in low-slung purple jeans with a bright yellow and orange plaid shirt, nodded his head. "Oh, we have a special mission today. We're going where we'll need the strength of a lion and the toughness of a rhinoceros, not to mention the endurance of a marathon runner."

Aiden looked at him curiously. "And that is…?" he asked.

Eric grinned. "To the mall!"

*   *   *

The large mall was busy with shoppers out to find the perfect purchase at the perfect price or just to check out the attractions that were a weekend feature. Aiden noted that this week, it was a child's petting zoo and parents were out in full force with their toddlers.

"So why did you drag me down here on a Saturday?" Aiden asked as they elbowed their way through the crowds.

"I just wanted to hang out and watch the groovy chicks go by!" Eric said, spinning in a circle.

"Right, and I'm here because I wanted to spend the day with an obnoxious runt." Aiden tried to make his voice sound sarcastic, but he found it came out more as a good-natured tease than a slam.

"Actually, my mom sent me down here to purchase new underwear as she is somewhat embarrassed by my fashion sense." Eric snapped the elastic on his pink boxers that were sticking out of his pants.

Aiden stopped and grabbed Eric by the shoulder. "We're what?" he asked, not believing what this nutcase had just told him.

Eric went on like this was nothing unusual. "Yeah, my mom gave me thirty bucks to buy several pairs of Stanfield's best."

Eric wore candy cane-striped sunglasses with mirrored lenses that reflected Aiden's startled face back at him. "Look, man, I don't buy no jockstraps with no guy. That's really uncool." He shook his head excitedly. "No way, Jose." The idea of shopping for something like *that* with the runt freaked Aiden out.

"*Any*," Eric said calmly.

"What?" Aiden asked, confused again.

"You don't buy *any* jockstraps and I don't either. My mom says to buy new undies, and I was thinking maybe glow in the dark…" He paused, then went on. "But instead, I'm going to get something way better that I've wanted for a long time." Eric was excited now.

Aiden was afraid to ask. "Like what?"

"I'm going to get my nose pierced or maybe my tongue! I haven't made up my mind yet. I'll see what strikes me when we get to the piercing parlour." He headed off whistling.

The idea of standing by while Eric got his tongue pierced was disgusting.

Aiden caught up. "Have you thought this through, Runt? Piercing your tongue is gross and way too painful for a Saturday, or any day for that matter." He snapped his fingers. "I've got it. Why don't you start out with something smaller — like your ears?"

Eric thought about this for a moment. "Hey, I could probably get both ears pierced for the price of one tongue! I'm down with that!" He held up his hand for Aiden to high-five him.

Aiden looked at the up-stretched hand and shook his head. "Get serious, you freak." He turned and headed for the ear-piercing shop.

Once inside the store, Aiden looked around for the clerk. He spotted her coming out of a back room. From her dead white skin and dyed black hair, Aiden knew she was into the Gothic scene.

"What can I do for you boys today?" she asked, snapping

her gum. She wore black lipstick, which Aiden thought looked extremely cool.

"I'm interested in having some piercing done," Eric said smiling.

"We have a special on navel rings today," the girl began.

"Ah, no, just some earrings to start with." Eric sounded a little nervous to Aiden.

The pale girl nodded and walked to the counter display, her high-heeled boots clicking on the floor tiles. "These are your choices. What will it be?" she asked with another loud snap of her gum.

Aiden walked over to the display and started to list off the different types of earrings available. "There are silver or gold studs, stainless steel hoops or gold ones," he began.

"Hey, what's going on here?" the girl asked. "Let your buddy choose for himself."

"My *buddy* is blind," Aiden began explaining. "He can't see the earrings."

The young clerk looked at Eric, then back at Aiden. "Does he want one in each ear or two in one ear?" she asked Aiden.

"Why don't you ask him?" Aiden shrugged.

The girl looked at Eric and asked in a loud voice, "Do...you...want...one..."

"He's blind, not deaf," Aiden interrupted, becoming annoyed with the girl.

"I'll have both ears done with gold studs, please," Eric said calmly.

"Suit yourself. Have a seat." She indicated a chair by the desk to which Aiden guided Eric.

The clerk picked up a nasty apparatus that looked something like a stainless steel gun and, snapping her gum one last time, walked toward Eric.

As they left the shop, Eric seemed pale to Aiden. "Are you okay?" he asked.

Eric wiped his forehead. "I have a very low pain threshold. That was nearly more than I could take, but it was for a good cause — my truly cool sense of fashion." He proudly flashed the new gold studs adorning his bright red ears.

"You belong in a zoo, you know that, Runt." Aiden was glad Eric hadn't seen that tattooing was available in the store, or there might have been some tense moments.

Eric suddenly looked a little deflated. "I wouldn't know. I've never been to a zoo."

Aiden was shocked. "You've never been to the zoo? You're kidding me!"

"Cross my throat and hope to choke!" Eric held his hand up like he was swearing on a bible. "My mom is, shall we say, a little overprotective. Maybe she worries the wild animals might suddenly break out and I'd get caught in the stampede. Maybe she doesn't like the smell. Who knows how a mother's mind works?" He grinned at Aiden. "She didn't even want me to come to the mall with you today except I convinced her you were under constant police surveillance, so if anything happened to me, you could call for backup."

"Thanks a lot. You make me sound like a gangster." Aiden was a little peeved at Eric's description. He suddenly had an idea. "You want to get to know some animals up close and personal?" he asked.

"Sure, what have you got in mind?" Eric was listening intently.

"Come on, you'll see." He thought of what he'd just said. "Oh, sorry, man. I meant *you'll find out*."

Eric stopped. "Aiden, you have to stop tiptoeing around the fact that you think I'm not normal because I can't see. I was *born* this way; to me *I am normal*. If you have to watch every word you say, we'll never have any fun." He reached out his hand. "Let me take your arm and you can guide me. It's a lot faster than me whacking my cane into every pedestrian in the mall."

Aiden let Eric hold onto his arm as they wended their way toward the petting zoo set up in the centre court of the mall. As they approached, Aiden could see a calf, a miniature horse and equally small donkey, sheep, llamas, ducks, geese, goats and a bunch of small pigs. There were also rabbits, chickens and other assorted small creatures for the kids to enjoy.

"This is really strange," Aiden said, looking at all the tots enjoying the baby animals. "We're going to be the oldest, not to mention tallest guys in here. The other brats are five years old, max."

He guided Eric into the enclosure and began letting him touch all the animals as he explained what each was. "This is a sheep," he said, putting Eric's hand on the fuzzy animal's head. "It has a thick coat and a nice face."

"Hey, this guy is really woolly," Eric exclaimed as he patted the sheep's back.

"Exactly!" Aiden said with a smile. They went to the next stall. "This is a miniature donkey. Did you know that farmers use these guys to guard their livestock? They can be really mean."

Eric felt the long ears, then ran his hands along the animal's neck and back, ending with its tail. "He feels cool, but he could use a little deodorant." Just then the donkey pulled his lips back from his teeth and brayed loudly. "Whoa there, young fella! I was just kidding. You smell great! Real outdoorsy. A true nose-pleaser." Eric shook his head. "Touchy!"

Next the boys explored the pigpen. Piglets were hard to

catch as Aiden found out when he unsuccessfully dived for one and ended up face down in the hay. Finally, he handed a squirming bundle to Eric.

"Hey, little dude, thanks for the BLT." Eric patted the smooth skin of the pig and, releasing the squealing animal, moved on to a large goose.

"Hey, Runt, you're talking to the wrong end of that thing." Aiden chuckled as he watched Eric exchanging pleasantries with the rump of the bird.

Eric stood up and Aiden went over to the next animal on their tour. "Here's a rabbit. He's kind of cute, if you're into that sort of thing," he remarked, handing the soft bundle to Eric.

Eric stood still for a long time, just patting the lop-eared bunny. "Not much of a talker, is he?"

"Maybe he's waiting for you to say something intelligent!" Aiden laughed, punching Eric on the shoulder and nearly knocking him into the stall with the cow.

"Very funny," Eric said, holding the rabbit out for Aiden to take.

When they had touched every animal in the zoo at least twice, Aiden noticed the time. "We'd better get going, Runt. It'll be dark soon."

Reluctantly, Eric left the enclosure, a sappy smile on his face. "Aiden, this has been the best day ever. And I don't just mean because I had my first body parts pierced, I'm talking about the Dr. Doolittle thing. I had no idea what these animals were really like. I mean I've read about them and had them described to me, but that's nothing compared to a little hands-on experience."

Suddenly feeling embarrassed at how grateful Eric was for such a simple thing, Aiden shrugged his shoulders. "It was nothing. Get over it, Runt." But he nudged Eric gently with his elbow so that the still-smiling boy could hold on as they headed out of the mall.

Once outside, Aiden noticed the temperature had fallen dramatically and it had started snowing. The heavy grey clouds looked so close that Aiden thought he could reach up and touch them. "Button up, Runt. It's going to be a cold walk. Let's go to the Anderson Station bus terminal and catch the number thirteen, then we won't have to change buses."

"Sounds good to me," Eric agreed. "This cold is making my new gold studs hum."

They left the bright lights of the mall and started toward the distant station. Aiden noticed how much darker the clouds made it seem.

They hadn't gone far when he thought he caught a flash of movement out of the corner of his eye. He turned to look, but there was no one behind them.

Ahead, Aiden could see a tunnel under the street they would have to take to get to the bus terminal. All the lights were out and the blackness made him shiver. If he were going to *straighten out* some wimp, this is the spot he'd pick.

"What's the matter, tough guy? Can't take a little cold?" Eric teased, feeling Aiden's tremor.

"No, Runt. We have to walk through a tunnel up ahead and there aren't any lights so it's really dark. It's just a little creepy, that's all." Aiden glanced around. They were completely alone.

"Yeah, so what else is new?" Eric chuckled. "I don't worry too much about whether the lights are on or not. Just stick with me and I'll get us through."

They'd gone a short distance into the black mouth of the tunnel, when Aiden heard a definite noise behind them. He whirled and saw a form silhouetted against the pale circle of light at the tunnel's entrance.

"You guys lost or something," the tall figure growled, then stepped closer so that Aiden could see his face.

He was a heavy-set teenager with greasy black hair pulled back in an untidy ponytail. His face was pockmarked and he looked tough.

Aiden heard the menace in the boy's voice. He knew what this guy was going to try to do. After all, Aiden was an expert when it came to bullying. "No, man. We're meeting some buddies of ours. They're coming over from the bus stop at Anderson." He knew that sounded weak, but if the guy thought help was not far away, maybe he'd leave them alone. He felt Eric stiffen at his side.

"I think that's a stinking lie," the big goon said, taking another step toward Aiden and Eric. "Why would a wimp like you want to lie to a nice guy like me?"

Aiden felt his blood starting to pound in his ears. He knew this feeling. "Look, we don't want any trouble," he said slowly, adrenaline making the hair on the back of his neck stand up.

"Well maybe I do," the big teenager said with a sneer. "You guys got any money on you?"

Aiden loosened his coat, allowing himself more freedom to maneuver. "Yeah, and I'm keeping it." He couldn't believe this creep. He had some nerve.

"We'll see about that," the big teen said with a raspy laugh.

Aiden took a step toward the goon. "You think so, punk? Well, bring it on."

Just then, two other guys jumped down from the bank on the sides of the tunnel's entrance where they'd been hiding and stood beside the leader.

"Oh crap," Aiden cursed under his breath. It would be tough to win with three against one odds. He could probably outrun these guys and make it to the safety of the bus terminal, but what about Eric? He couldn't leave him behind. But if he stayed and they pounded him, what would happen to Eric then? These guys weren't going to let his buddy go.

Aiden suddenly felt protective of the blind boy he had come to like because he realized that was what had happened somewhere between the ear-piercing and the goat patting. He actually *liked* Eric. "Get behind me, Runt," he said, his voice deadly calm. If these punks wanted a fight, he'd give them one. This was something he knew and did well.

Aiden casually shook off the thick mitts he was wearing and took a step forward. His hands were clenched into tight fists. He might be able to take these guys, but it was going to be messy.

"Don't worry. I'll call for backup," Eric said, fumbling in his pocket. He took out his cell phone and tried to turn it on. "Rats! I forgot to charge the battery," he said a little nervously. "Wait till my mom hears about this. She'll never let me forget."

Aiden suddenly remembered the cell phone Michael had given him. He pulled the small phone out of his jacket and flipped it open. He hit the auto dial for Michael and handed the phone to Eric without taking his eyes off the three thugs. "Tell Michael what's going on and where we are, then start moving to the far end of the tunnel, get to the bus station and stay there," he instructed. It was funny to think the first time he was using the phone was not because he was doing the bullying, but because he was being bullied. It felt strange to be on the receiving end of the fist.

The three boys started edging closer.

Aiden heard Eric whispering quickly into the phone. He breathed a sigh of relief. Now all he had to do was stall the inevitable until Michael showed up. Aiden figured he had about five minutes, tops, then he'd have no choice. The odds were not good, but these guys must be real chickens if all three were going to attack him at one time.

"You three have nothing better than to pick on one guy? You really are wimps." He looked from the big guy to his smaller buddies. "You don't have to do this. If you want to pound someone, I'd be happy to oblige. I haven't had a good scrap in weeks and could use the practice. My friend here had nothing to do with it. He should be out of this." Aiden could hear Eric stuffing the phone in his pocket. Then he heard the familiar sound of Eric's white cane being snapped open.

Eric stepped up beside Aiden. "All for one, and one for all!" He held the cane out in front of him like a knight with a sword.

"You two are freaking nuts!" the biggest goon said, his eyes narrowing as he stared at the two boys. Then his face broke into a slow, dangerous smile. "But that ain't going to save you." He nodded his head and all three thugs started closing in on Aiden and Eric.

8

New Team, Old Tricks

Aiden glared at the three boys, who were edging closer. He could tell these bullies were used to picking on easy targets. He felt a wave of guilt wash over him. He was good at pushing weaker kids around, too. That was how he'd always handled things, with his fists.

Aiden could see himself doing exactly what this tough guy was doing. If he had the choice to straighten a jerk out or leave him alone, he always chose his fists. Charlie had taught him it was right to put punks in their place, especially weak, wimpy punks. But now that he was the one being picked on and more importantly, Eric was also a target, things looked a lot different.

Aiden thought about it and decided Eric wouldn't stand a chance. He wasn't a fighter; instead, he liked to talk a problem to pieces. He seemed to be able to understand both sides and it made it a lot harder to fight when you saw things from the other guy's angle. This time there was no choice. Aiden had to fight. He began planning his strategy, deciding to take the leader out first. There was a good chance the other two would run once the head jerk was flattened.

He could feel his heart thumping in his chest. One thing was for sure, if they got through him, they would go for Eric. Glancing over at the skinny kid standing by his side and armed with only his white cane, Aiden knew he was going to have to make sure that didn't happen. Taking a deep breath, he gathered his muscles, ready to spring at the leader.

Suddenly, the blinding glare of a powerful flashlight illuminated the dark tunnel in brilliant, white light.

"Aiden, Eric, are you boys in there?" It was Michael.

The three thugs looked at the light moving toward them. "Run!" the biggest bully yelled as all three began sprinting to the far end of the underpass.

Michael hurried to the boys, breathless. "Are you okay?" he asked, looking from one to the other.

Aiden glanced at Eric. He still held his white cane as though it were a magic sword. His hand was steady and he looked ready to defend himself no matter what the odds. "From the look of my well-armed friend here," he jerked a thumb at Eric, "we could have handled it, no sweat."

"Those cowards never stood a chance," Eric said bravely. "My buddy and I could have creamed them with our eyes closed!"

Michael drove both boys home, dropping Eric off first. "Pretty scary stuff," he said, climbing back in the car after helping Eric to his door.

"Yeah, but I wasn't worried. I could have taken that big mouth." Aiden felt a lot surer sitting here in Michael's warm car. "You straight-arrow types may not like my style of handling things, but my fists have taken care of a lot of punks like those three. *Straightening out* those jerks was the only way to handle a situation like that." The more he talked, the tougher he felt.

Michael sighed. "Fighting is what you're used to, so it's the first thing you think of doing, but there's always another way, like talking or avoiding the situation in the first place. Today you did the very best thing you could have done. You got adult help, my help, and I was glad to give it. Sometimes when you see something you know is wrong, you should step up and make it right. That's being brave. But, there are times when you should let the little things go *because you are the strong one and you can choose to walk away*. Remember, win or lose, sometimes the consequences are just too big."

He shook his head. "What if you hadn't succeeded in taking all three of those guys? I'm not sure how well Eric would have done." He glanced over at Aiden. "It was a good thing you were there to protect him. Eric's not used to fighting and because he can't see, he always feels a little vulnerable."

Aiden realized what Michael was getting at. Ordinarily, Eric would make a good target, especially if a guy just wanted to hit something because he was mad. The small blind kid would have made a convenient punching bag to work off a little steam. He thought about the way he'd felt when those three creeps had been making their move. He had been worried, not for himself, but for Eric, who had stood with him when he could have run away. He didn't have to do that. It wasn't like they were friends or anything, right? "Nothing happened to the runt, because I can fight; I would have taken care of those punks."

"You're missing the point," Michael said quietly. "If those guys hadn't picked on you in the first place, you wouldn't have had to worry about fighting at all."

Aiden looked down at his hands. "I would have looked after him," he mumbled. "Picking on a kid like Eric just isn't cool."

He went straight up to his room after Michael dropped him off. He had a lot to think about, then he wanted to phone his mom. He needed to talk to her.

*   *   *

The following Saturday, Michael came to pick Aiden up.

Eric was with him. "You need to bring your hockey gear," he said, hanging out the car window and yelling at Aiden as he was coming out of his house. "I've got another practice and you might as well skate instead of sitting on your butt."

Aiden stopped and stared at Eric. He thought of the humiliating experience that he'd had the first time he'd skated with the Seeing Ice Dogs. That was one hockey experience he didn't want to repeat. "No way." He shook his head stubbornly. "I'm not playing with that bunch of losers again. I don't like it when people use me as a joke." He had a small twinge of guilt as he thought of the number of times he'd teased some kid and made him feel like an idiot, but this was different. This time he was the one who'd been made to look like a geek. He crossed his arms and waited.

Eric pursed his lips as though thinking about this unexpected turn of events. "Two things," he began. "One, the guys do that to every new skater. They do it to make sure everyone tries as hard as they can. We don't want or need any special favours because we're blind. It's their way of saying it's okay to go for the gold. And two…" He paused, then pushed his silver wrap-around sunglasses farther up the bridge of his nose. "I hate to pull rank, but on Saturdays, I'm the captain." He wiggled back into the car and rolled up the window before Aiden had a chance to say anything.

Muttering under his breath, Aiden went back to get his equipment.

*   *   *

The rink was busy. There were skaters everywhere doing their warm-up drills when the boys hit the ice.

"Hey, you came back," Kevin Gardner said with a smile as he skated toward Eric and Aiden. "We were a little worried we'd scared you off."

Gary Zarbock was holding onto Kevin's arm as he was escorted to his goal. "Great to have you on the team, Aiden. We have a big game coming up and can use all the talent we can get."

"You've got the wrong idea," Aiden shouted to the retreating goalie. "I'm only here because I have to be. The runt is a real baby when it comes to getting his own way."

"Thanks a lot, loser," Eric said, as he reached out and first touched, then punched, Aiden on the shoulder.

Aiden, ignoring the feeble hit, tightened the strap on his white helmet. "Come on, let's get this over with." He moved to centre ice for the faceoff.

"You'll be playing with us," Eric said. "We're the Good Guys, which makes the other team the Bad Guys."

"You're all *Loser Guys* if you ask me," Aiden grumbled, taking his position. Today he'd be playing left defence with Kevin on right while Eric was a left forward and Jeff Galbraith the other winger. Rod Rogalsky was their centre and Gary would be in goal. The other squad, the Bad Guys, lined up ready to steamroll Aiden's team.

As the puck dropped, Rod slapped it out to Kevin who passed it up ice toward Jeff, but before Jeff could snag the puck, Ian Richardson, the red helmeted forward for the Bad Guys, scooped it and turned toward the goal.

Aiden cut hard across the rink to intercept Ian, a surprisingly fast skater, who had Danny Dawes, a sighted skater, calling out the play to him.

"Aiden's coming up fast on your right," Danny called. "Al's up ahead on your left about five metres with a clear shot on goal." Using a backhand pass, Ian slid it smoothly to Al Laughlin, who picked it up, spun and shot.

It should have worked, except for some of the fanciest stick-handling by a goalie that Aiden had ever seen. Gary was somehow able to detect where the puck was, snag it on his stick and pass it back out the other side of the goal crease to Jeff, who had come in to get the rebound.

Jeff turned and headed back down ice. Aiden had to hustle to keep up. He saw Brandon moving up to strip the puck from Jeff. Aiden moved in and checked him right out of the play, being careful not to *over-muscle* the guy. Eric had been right. It was tougher to check skillfully. The big skater spun around, but by that time Jeff was in the slot. He wound up and fired one at the bottom right corner. Wham! Clean goal!

All the players cheered like it had been the winner at the gold medal round in the Olympics.

"Great job, Aiden," Eric called. "I heard you check Brandon on that last play!"

"Nice check!" Brandon said, rubbing his shoulder and smiling at Aiden. "You're tough!"

The other players congratulated him on his great effort. Aiden felt good about his check. He'd done it just right.

On their next break, everyone crowded into the players' box. "Hey, Aiden, as the new guy, you have a fresh look on things. Can you see anything we can do to improve our game?" Eric asked as he took a long drink of water.

Aiden had seen a couple of things that might help, but he hadn't wanted to say anything. "Yeah, but nobody would want to hear what I've got to say."

"The Seeing Ice Dogs don't work like that. We're *old dogs*, but we like learning *new tricks*. What have you got?" Eric asked.

Aiden looked around. He wasn't used to being treated like he was more than muscle. "Okay," he began, still hesitating.

"Come on, Aiden, we have to finish this game *today*!" Eric prompted.

Aiden took a deep breath and began. "One way we can lessen the other guys' chances is to protect our middle lane, that strip of ice that ends up between our goalposts. We should keep the Bad Guys wide against the boards. Another basic is to keep no more than two stick lengths between you and your check. Then you're right on top of the play if the guy gets the puck."

He turned to Gary, who was listening intently. "Gary, you're wicked between the pipes. You seemed to know exactly where the puck was and where the guy was going to shoot. How do you do it?"

Gary shrugged his shoulders. "Call it a gift!" he laughed.

"I doubt there's any way you could improve on your moves. You obviously remember the basics; be aware of where your stick is on the ice, no holes near your posts, and use your angles to cut down the available open net area."

"Always good advice," Gary agreed.

"That's it. If I think of anything else, I'll let you know," Aiden finished.

When his squad hit the ice for the last period, they tried a couple of Aiden's suggestions and the plays did move faster. Both Eric and Jeff scored. The Good Guys were very happy as they left the ice but what amazed Aiden was the Bad Guys were equally cheerful. They had all played well and enjoyed themselves.

Aiden showered and changed into his street clothes, then went to wait for Michael to take him home. Eric came up behind him, tapping him lightly with his cane. "We're going out for burgers and beer." He slapped Aiden on the back and laughed loudly. "Root beer, that is, and the guys sent me out to make sure you were coming." He became serious. "I'd really like it if you came."

Aiden heard the sincerity in his voice and remembered how good he'd felt playing with the Seeing Ice Dogs. "Michael is supposed to be picking me up," he said lamely.

Eric turned and started back to the dressing room. "So, call him on the fancy phone he gave you and tell him to scoop you up at the Burger Barn instead."

When the team arrived at the restaurant, everyone was in a great mood. There was a lot of joking and laughing and Aiden sat and listened. Aiden had never wanted to go out with the Devils after a game. The fact that they never asked him might have had something to do with his not wanting to go. He'd never cared before, but now he wondered if it was like this when the Devils went out. Everyone joked and praised each other's playing, including his. This experience was new and he liked it.

"You should play in the NHL, Aiden. You're really good," Brian Clark, the other Ice Dog goalie, said, as he squirted ketchup in the vicinity of his fries.

"Or do something really important, like coach," Randy added as he took a bite out of his third hamburger.

Aiden thought of how the Devils' coach played him strictly for his muscle and how Charlie would tell him he'd done a good job only after he'd creamed some kid into the boards. Today, he'd played hard but hadn't checked anyone hard enough to raise a bruise and these guys still thought he was some kind of star. Aiden smiled to himself as the guys continued praising him.

"If you don't stop, he'll never be able to get his hockey helmet on over that swelled head," Eric laughed, launching a punch at Aiden's shoulder.

Aiden, who was just about to take a bite out of his hamburger, felt it fly out of his hand. Eric's punch was a little off the mark. The burger flew across the table and landed on Kevin Gardner's plate.

"Hey, he shoots; he scores!" Kevin yelled as he tried to fire the burger back using only a long french fry. "I need a better trapper if I'm going into the goaltending business. Gary, give me your carrot stick, and a bigger french fry, there's too much gravy on this one and it's gone soggy."

"You need more of a celery stalk to stop anything as big as a burger, Kev," Gary said, reaching over and removing the burger from Kevin's plate. "Or I could be the goal judge and call no goal." He grinned and promptly took a huge bite out of the burger, chewing happily.

"Great job, Gary, except that was my burger," Aiden said, surprised that he felt no anger.

"Talk to Eric. He started this." Gary held out his plate. "Or you can take mine. I seem to have a couple!"

Everyone laughed as Aiden took the spare burger and began munching on it, keeping a safe distance from Eric.

On the ride home, Aiden told Michael all about the shinny game and how the Good Guys had won. Michael was impressed with all the great strategies Aiden had come up with. "It sounds like you've got real talent. I'm going to have to come out and see you play with the Devils."

Aiden felt his spirits soar, but his elation soon evaporated. If Michael came out to see him play, all he'd watch was an enforcer tearing kids apart on the ice.

*   *   *

"What's the matter, boy? That wimp you babysit giving you a headache?" Charlie asked when Aiden walked into the living room.

Aiden was still thinking about how Michael would only get to see him as muscle, but he could not tell his dad this. "No, actually, I had a great time this afternoon. I played with the Seeing Ice Dogs and I came up with some great plays. The guys think I should have more goal-scoring action or maybe even help with some player coaching."

"Let's not start that up again. Those guys don't know what they're talking about. They're blind, for Pete's sake. Think about it, Aiden. To be a high scorer you need quick reflexes, above-average stickhandling and especially a sharpshooter's eye. They don't play real hockey, so they're not in a position to judge." Charlie went back to reading the paper.

"I'm not saying they play Olympic gold-level hockey," Aiden started to protest. "They play fun hockey. This afternoon I really liked…"

Charlie cut him off. "I left your supper on the stove. Help yourself," he said without looking up.

"I had burgers with the Ice Dogs after practice," Aiden mumbled, as he headed out of the room.

Charlie looked up in surprise. "That's not like you, boy. You don't usually like to hang out with wimps."

Aiden thought of all the things he and Eric had done, like their encounter with the thugs when Eric had stood fearlessly by his side. He remembered how he was prepared to fight to protect the blind boy. He also thought about playing for the Seeing Ice Dogs and how good that had made him feel. "Yeah, well, lately I've been doing a lot of stuff that's *not like me*." Aiden trudged upstairs feeling confused.

9

A Change of Tactics

Sometimes things change and you don't even realize it until it's too late. Aiden felt different as he suited up in his Devils' uniform for a game against the Southside Thunder, but he wasn't sure why. This was an important game. If they beat the Thunder, they'd take first place in the league standings, which would be sweet. They'd never been in first place before or beaten the Thunder.

As Aiden dressed, he found himself thinking that he really didn't feel much like spending three periods pounding some kid's face into the ice. This was different for him; usually, he could hardly wait to start slicing and dicing. If the coach would just let him in on a few scoring attempts, it wouldn't be so bad. Maybe he'd even see how good Aiden was at sucking goalies out of their socks and let him play something other than meat grinder.

Jamie was sitting on a bench busily adjusting the laces on his skates. He looked up as Aiden walked past. Aiden stopped and was going to say something to his old friend, but couldn't find the right words.

"Have a good game," Jamie said, then went back to his laces.

Aiden nodded and resumed walking. Lately, Jamie hadn't

talked much to him, except to argue or give him grief. This sudden friendliness was unexpected.

They'd always missed beating the Thunder by one or two goals. Today the Devils had to pull off a win. Everyone on the team knew this was going to be a tough game and they came out ready to fight.

The game was fast and furious with both sides racking up goal after goal, but neither pulling far enough in front to secure a safe lead. The Thunder was *not* a tough physical team, relying instead on slick plays, great puck control and fast skating. Aiden had always thought their shying away from physical showdowns proved they were a bunch of weak wimps and he liked to get them running scared by grinding a couple of their players into the ice right at the beginning of the game. They quickly got the message and would waste a lot of time looking over their shoulders for him. This was one team that could bleed.

Aiden looked down ice and saw a Thunder forward waiting to receive the pass from their centre. The kid was trying to sneak down the outside to catch Todd Roche, the Devil goalie, off guard.

As if, Aiden thought, turning to start his run at the unsuspecting forward. He would come in fast, low and hard like a supersonic guided missile. He tightened his grip with both hands on his stick. Lowering his centre of gravity over his skates, he was about to hammer the guy, when he suddenly slowed, and turning, shoulder checked him instead. The forward, caught unprepared, was spun out of position to receive the pass. Aiden waited for the usual whistle signalling another trip to the penalty box, but it never came.

In the crease, Todd was concentrating on the Thunder centre, who had the puck and was now steaming toward him.

Aiden started after the centre. Out of the corner of his eye, he saw Jamie moving toward the puckhandler. Jamie nodded and together, they moved in on the Thunder centre, crowding him into the boards. There was a scrum as the centre tried to elbow his way out from between Jamie and Aiden. Aiden pinned the guy so Jamie could take the puck, then released him. Again Aiden waited for the whistle, but the refs never even looked at him.

Jamie smoked down to the Thunder end, flew around the goalpost and tossed in the sweetest wraparound Aiden had ever seen. The crowd went wild as the scoreboard read seven all.

The Thunder dug in and put on a dazzling show of skating prowess and great plays. They fired a dozen shots on goal, but Todd held on. Several times, Aiden could have creamed a Thunder skater, but instead, he'd checked him hard enough to take him out of the play, but not hard enough to draw a penalty. It was odd not to hear whistles every time he hit a player. With only minutes left in the third period and the score tied, Aiden found himself the only Devil player in their own end.

"*Two on one!*" Todd shouted to Aiden as the two Thunder forwards stripped the puck from Jamie and headed toward the Devil net at full speed.

Aiden concentrated on the Thunder forward who would be the pass receiver. If the pass came, it would be Aiden's job to intercept it. He left the Devil goalie to handle the other guy. Usually, he'd steamroll the guy and take him out, but if he pulled a penalty now, the Devils would have to play the last couple of minutes short-handed. It was too big a risk. He moved deep into Devil territory, covering the open forward as he and his teammate moved in to attack Todd.

Once the Thunder skaters were in close, Aiden knew that Todd would stack his pads to block the shot and the deflection would be redirected out to him. He glanced around and saw his teammates were still too far away to help.

The puckhandler tried to deke Aiden out with a fake pass, then headed straight for the Devil goal. Aiden moved in close and got ready for the rebound. The shot was on target, but deflected off Todd's pads and out to Aiden, just like he knew it would.

He was ready. Scooping the puck with his stick, Aiden flashed past his teammates, who had caught up, and started back down to the Thunder's end. He could hear the crowd cheering the breakaway as the clock ticked down.

Up ahead he saw the two Thunder defencemen moving toward him. He could try to out-muscle them and take the puck in himself, but if he lost control, they would be able to take it back down ice and rush the Devils' undefended net. Aiden knew by now Todd would have been pulled and on his way to the bench, allowing the Devils to put an extra forward on the ice, which would be great once Aiden had the puck in that end. His job was to get it there safely.

As he crossed the blue line, Aiden saw Jamie streak past and set himself up at the far side of the hash marks, near the Thunder goal. He was in the clear. Aiden really wanted to score himself, but with those two big defencemen heading right for him, his chances of getting a good shot on goal were slim.

He took a deep breath and puffed it out through his facemask. Aiden wanted the Devils to win and he realized he had to do whatever it took to make that happen. Without hesitating, he fired a hard flip pass to Jamie, who turned and slammed in a super fast wrist shot. The goal light whirled! The horn sounded, ending the game. The Devils had won, thanks to Jamie's great shot.

Aiden turned and began skating slowly over to the Devils'

bench. He'd wanted to score that goal, to be the one the crowd was cheering for. However, the good part was that the Devils had won and were now the number-one team in the league.

He was just about at the gate, when Jamie skated up from behind.

Spinning Aiden around, Jamie grabbed his gloved hand and raised it above both their heads. "We did it! We won! You were great!" Jamie yelled, grinning through his mask at Aiden.

Aiden looked up at the stands and realized the fans were cheering for him, too. He and Jamie were the heroes of the game. He looked at the boy who used to be his friend. "*We* were great!" he corrected, grinning at Jamie. "All right, Devils!" he cheered, waving his stick in the air as he saluted the fans.

The celebration continued in the dressing room. Everyone slapped him on the back and said what a great job he'd done.

Coach Goldstein smiled at Aiden. "You put on quite the show out there, Aiden. You picked off those Thunder players perfectly. I liked the way you put the good of the team before anything else." He nodded thoughtfully as though he were seeing Aiden in a whole new light. "We're going to have to talk about using your other talents. You and Jamie would make a high-scoring team."

Aiden watched him walk away. That had been a strange conversation, great, but strange.

Jamie clumped over, still in his skates, and plunked down next to Aiden. "Do you realize you spent less time in the penalty box this game than any in the past two years?" He smiled at Aiden.

Aiden didn't say anything.

"Don't you get it? You didn't have to be the big gun and blow everyone to smithereens to do your job. You used just the right amount of muscle tonight and you did it legally. The refs could have taken the night off!" He laughed.

Aiden realized that what Jamie said was true. He had skated much more in this game and sat a lot less. His legs were aching to prove it. "I guess that's right," Aiden said, trying to sound cool. He began pulling off his skates and wiping the blades down, and deep down, he suddenly felt very good.

"We're going out to celebrate. You coming?" Jamie asked, taking Aiden's cloth and wiping his own skate blades dry.

Aiden didn't know what to say. Everything in his world seemed to be changing and it made him feel a little confused. He needed to think about things, especially the way he'd played and felt tonight. This was all too strange. "Ah, I'll take a rain check. My dad's waiting for me. I have to go."

Jamie handed him back the cloth. "Then, maybe we could get together sometime and just, you know, hang out?" He looked at Aiden expectantly.

Aiden nodded at him. "Sure." He didn't know what else to say. "I still have your phone number," he added. "I'll call."

"Great!" Jamie said as he stood up and headed out of the dressing room.

Several other players came over to congratulate Aiden on a super game. They thought he'd played great. "It was a real team effort," he'd answered, feeling a little embarrassed and nodding his head at the unaccustomed praise. Aiden finished dressing and went out to meet Charlie. He was happy about patching things up with Jamie. Aiden had missed his friendship.

Charlie was waiting for him just inside the doors to the arena and he didn't look happy. His arms were folded across his chest and he had an expression on his face that meant trouble. The last time he'd seen that expression, Charlie had been turfed from the Rose Kohn Arena for yelling at a coach after a game.

Aiden was surprised to see Michael standing next to him.

He must have meant it when he said he wanted to see Aiden play with the Devils. Usually people just say stuff like that to be polite. The two men looked so different, his dad, big, bulky and bald and Michael, short, slight and looking very Indian with his dark hair and skin.

Michael was dressed casually, which was not how Aiden was used to seeing him. He had on blue jeans and a buckskin coat with a brightly coloured flower design worked in beads across the back and down the front. Michael seemed oblivious to the fact that he was wearing what amounted to a beautiful bouquet of flowers on his jacket. Aiden doubted Charlie had failed to notice.

He walked over to the two men and dropped his equipment bag on the floor. "What did you think of the game? Wasn't it great?" Aiden asked, still feeling elated from his experience in the dressing room with Jamie, the coach and the rest of the guys. He felt like he'd finally been accepted as one of them and not just the goon on skates.

"What the hell do you think you were doing out there tonight, boy?" Charlie exploded, ignoring Michael.

"Ah, I, I…" Aiden stuttered. He hadn't expected this anger after how everyone else had reacted. He wasn't sure what to say to make Charlie happy.

"You were skating like some kind of wimpy freaking girl! I couldn't believe how you let those losers off. Any punk from the street could have done a better job than you did!" His face was bright red and he was waving his arms around like a mad-man.

"I thought he played with skill and good sportsmanship," Michael said, interrupting Charlie's tirade and nodding at Aiden. "And from what I know about hockey, I'd say Aiden's staying on the ice defending his teammates was a more effective method of playing than spending half the night in the penalty box for cross-checking or high-sticking."

Charlie turned on Michael, his eyes flashing dangerously. "*From what you know about hockey!* Just what is it that you think you know that I don't?" He poked a finger in Michael's chest. "I've been teaching this boy for years how to take care of himself on the ice and off. Everyone knows he's a force to be reckoned with. *Just ask them!*"

Michael never flinched. Instead, he looked Charlie straight in the eye. "Oh, I have, Mr. Walsh."

"Come on, boy," Charlie snarled. "I need some fresh air." He took Aiden's big hockey bag and stalked out of the arena.

Aiden looked helplessly at Michael, then hurriedly followed.

When they were in the truck, Charlie let out a big breath and shook his head. "You really didn't play very tough hockey tonight, boy. Was something the matter? Are you sick?" He turned out of the parking lot and headed to their favourite all-you-can-eat-buffet restaurant.

"I was trying something different," Aiden explained. "I learned it playing with the Seeing Ice Dogs. It turns out it really is harder to be an enforcer who stays *out* of the penalty box than one who spends half his shifts *in*."

"Well, *different* stinks! And whatever you think you learned from that loser team, that stinks, too. You can't let those jerks run over you." He ran his hand over his smooth head. "Look, Aiden, I know what it's like to have someone continually stomp you into the ground because they think they're tougher than you. When I was your age I was on the receiving end of more than my share. When I think of the number of times I went home with a bloody nose and ripped shirt only to have my old man straighten me out for not sticking up for myself." He shook his head. "I don't want you to be in that position. I want you to show them they can't push you around. You're king of the turf." He pulled into the parking lot of the restaurant and parked. "The world is made up of two kinds of people, boy, winners and losers. I want you to be a winner and if it means kicking some loser butt, I'm okay with that!" He smiled at his son.

"I know you want the best for me, Charlie, but lately, I've come to think that kicking loser butt all the time isn't okay with me." Aiden rubbed the birthmark on his neck, arranging his thoughts. "It seems like I'm always the outsider. Sometimes I just want to go through a day without having to shove some kid into the lockers at school or smash a hockey player into the boards because that's what's expected of me and if I don't, people will think I've gone soft." He looked at his father. "I want people to respect me because of who I am and how well I do things, not because they're afraid of what I'll do to them."

His dad shook his head. "You don't understand the way the real world works, boy. When you get older, you'll see your old man was right. The only way not to be pushed around is to be the one doing the pushing!" He reached into the glove compartment and took out a box. "I picked this up for you. You nagged so long, I thought I'd get you one just to shut you up. Besides, the toughest hitter in the league deserves a little reward."

Aiden opened the box. It was the latest hand-held super video game called GameBox. He *had* wanted it, badly, but he hadn't thought Charlie was paying attention when he'd dropped all those hints. "Wow! Thanks, Charlie! This is the exact one I wanted." He smiled at his dad, forgetting what he'd just said. Sometimes, Charlie was the greatest!

"I just wanted to let you know I understand how hard it is to be the tough guy and that it doesn't matter what any of those whiners say. Why don't you bring it with you into the restaurant? We can have a game to see who pays the bill!" Charlie said, slapping Aiden on the back.

Aiden put the game into his coat pocket and, smiling, went into the restaurant with his dad.

10

New Friends Are Sometimes Hard to See

Aiden could hardly wait for eight o'clock to come, so he could fire up his computer and tell his mom all about last night's game. She would be proud of him. He also wanted to tell Eric about his new GameBox, but that would have to wait till the weekend. It was unusual for Charlie to get him a present for no special reason and Christmas was still a couple of weeks away. He'd said he just wanted Aiden to have it, no strings or occasions attached, but he had also said it was a pat on the back for being a tough guy on the ice.

At eight o'clock, he turned on his computer, found the camera icon, selected his mom's IP address and hit *dial*. She must have been waiting for his call, because she answered it right away. He noticed her face in the tiny window on the computer screen was beaming, as though she knew some big secret that would rock his world.

"How did the game go?" she asked. "I know it was an important one."

He nodded enthusiastically. "Mom, you should have been there! The Devils won in a squeaker that had us scrambling right down to the wire. Jamie pulled off the winning goal and we were all heroes, including yours truly," he added proudly.

"Why? What happened?" his mom asked as she took a sip of tea from a delicate china cup. It was the one Aiden had given her last Christmas. He went on to tell her all about his new style of playing that involved more skill and far less penalties. He also told her what the coach had said and that he and Jamie were going to hang out.

Smiling warmly, his mom nodded her head. "Oh, honey, I am so pleased to hear this. It sounds like things are turning around for you."

Aiden hadn't thought about this, but lately a lot of good things had happened. Usually, he had a lot more bad stuff in his life than good. He remembered his new GameBox. "Wait a minute," he said, leaving the computer and retrieving the video game from his coat pocket. "Charlie got me this." He held the video game in front of the camera. "Pretty cool, huh? It's the exact one I wanted and I can buy zillions of additional cartridges so I can play for years!" His dark eyes twinkled.

"That looks very impressive. It's odd your father never waited for Christmas to give it to you." There was a hint of reservation in her voice as though she was suspicious as to why Charlie had given him the game. It wasn't like his dad to give presents without a reason, such as making up for something he'd done.

Aiden frowned when he thought of what his dad said about having to push people around to survive. Then Michael's words came back to him. He had said there was always another way of handling a problem besides his fists. He was starting to get used to not using his fists to solve everything. Maybe Charlie was wrong this time and he didn't have to pound the world into submission. Maybe Charlie had been wrong about a lot of things.

"I guess he felt sorry for me because I've had to give up all my Saturdays with this community service thing." Aiden didn't want to tell his mom the GameBox was a reward for being a goon.

"How's that going? You said you thought this blind team was pretty neat. You seem to like Eric." She set her cup down somewhere out of camera range.

"Eric is really a great kid and Mom, he can play killer hockey. I've been skating with the Seeing Ice Dogs at a couple of practices, and those guys are unbelievable. They skate, stickhandle, shoot and check like you wouldn't believe. It's a lot of fun playing with them. I even went out for burgers and had a great time." He told her all about his adventures with the blind team. She seemed very pleased that he was enjoying the unique experience.

"And now, I have a surprise for you also," she said with a mischievous grin. "Guess who came to live with me today?"

Aiden had no idea and shrugged his shoulders.

"This little guy!" She held a squirming bundle of black fur in front of the camera. "He's my new buddy. One day he'll grow up big and strong to protect me. Won't you, cutie?" she asked, nuzzling the small puppy. "He's an eight-week-old Labrador retriever. I thought you might like to give him a name."

Aiden stared at the image on the computer screen. The little dog was all black with a tail that never stopped wagging and a tiny pink tongue, which was busy licking his mom's face. He was the cutest puppy Aiden had ever seen. "Mom, are you kidding me? Is he really yours?"

"Actually, the papers say he belongs to *Aiden Walsh.* I thought you were old enough to have a dog." A shadow crossed her face. "I know how your dad feels, so this little guy will live with me for now and you can visit him every weekend." Her face brightened and she smiled into the camera. "Okay, what are you going to call him?"

Aiden understood it was hard for his mom to see him only once a week. That was another mistake he'd made and now had to live with. He dismissed those gloomy thoughts and concentrated, staring out his bedroom window at the cold December night. The trees were white and tiny ice crystals winked at him as they swirled down out of the blackness. "Frost," he said with a smile. "We'll call him Frost!"

His mom's eyebrows went up in surprise. "You realize he'll stay black when he grows up."

"I know, but I think it's a cool name and sometimes what you see isn't the most important thing. Don't sweat the small stuff, Mom. He's a winter pup and Frost is a winter pup's name. If you'd never seen him, you'd think Frost was a great name." His words sounded strange, especially the part about not sweating the small stuff because he was a guy who did worry about little things — like kids looking at him wrong or some punk saying something he thought was a put-down. He was always on guard, almost waiting for an excuse to hit someone. Lately, he hadn't noticed things as much. Now *not sweating the small stuff* made sense.

His mom laughed. "When you put it that way, Frost is perfect!" she agreed. They began talking about the things they'd do with the pup as he grew. Finally, Aiden broke the connection, feeling better than he had in a long time.

*   *   *

On Saturday, Aiden and Eric were going to a special exhibit. It was the Canadian Hockey Display, a hockey museum on wheels. This mobile exhibit held all kinds of hockey memorabilia, such as Gretzky jerseys and sticks and equipment once worn by other superstars, as well as photos and lots of information.

All the way there Aiden talked animatedly about his new GameBox, explaining why it was the best and what cartridges he was going to buy. "And I can expand it so two can play, which makes it even more fun. There are games like Jet Plane Dog Fight and Stock Car Racing, where two players go head to head." He stopped, suddenly realizing how that must sound to Eric, who could never play a video game. Then he thought of himself and the fact he had no one to play with either. He was stunned to realize that he'd spent more time with Eric than any other kid his age in months. Aiden was glad when the bus pulled up to their stop and he could change subjects.

As the boys walked through the one-of-a-kind exhibit, Aiden explained each jersey and read all the information aloud to Eric. They were impressed with the amount of history the game had and what it meant to Canada.

"Hockey's been a part of Canada for a long time," Eric agreed, marvelling at each new tidbit of information. "In fact, it's believed that hockey began in the early 1800s in Windsor, Nova Scotia, at a place called Long Pond. It was played with wooden pucks, one-piece hockey sticks and stones for goal-posts. One of the earliest rubber pucks is said to have come from Montreal in the late 1870s."

Aiden shook his head, then realized what he was doing. "No kidding!" he said out loud, impressed with how much hockey history Eric knew.

"Oh, I could go on for hours. My gigantic brain is stuffed with all kinds of important junk." His voice was very serious, but Aiden could see he was trying not to laugh.

"That's true, you're definitely full of something!" Aiden agreed with a shake of his head. "But you really do know a lot of stuff, Runt."

"Yes, and not all of it based on survival, which was the focus of most of my extracurricular training." He went on speaking in that annoying way he had, kind of like a grade-six teacher lecturing a class. "When I was little, I went to a special school for the blind where they taught me important social skills like how to tell when to stop pouring your soda or how to dress like a normal person. I do okay on feeding myself and I opted to raise the bar on stylish clothes, but I always was ahead of my time."

Aiden glanced over at Eric incredulously. His magenta corduroy pants and lemon turtleneck with navy blue and lime green plaid vest weren't what was usually considered fashionable clothes for a normal person, but somehow, they suited Eric.

After they had thoroughly read and re-read every item in the displays, the boys reluctantly decided it was time to head for home. As they were leaving, a young boy accidentally bumped into Aiden as he entered the exhibit.

"Sorry," the young boy said, shoving past Aiden.

"Hey, guess what?" Aiden said, not even noticing the hit until Eric stiffened. Aiden sensed Eric's sudden tenseness. "What?" he asked, then glanced at the pushy kid's retreating back. "Oh, that? That was nothing. Don't sweat the small stuff, Runt."

Eric waited a couple of seconds, then shook his head. "I can hardly believe my ears!"

Aiden shrugged his shoulders and went on talking excitedly. "My mom got a puppy." He was just going to say how cute and cuddly the little guy was, when he thought of how un-cool that would sound. "It's an okay mutt," he said casually. "He's a black Lab and his name is Frost. At first my mom thought his name was dumb because he was all black and frost is white, but I didn't care. It suited him." Aiden thought about the fact that

Eric would have no idea of what black or green or red looked like because he'd never seen colours. There was no way he could describe a colour to Eric. How could he?

"Hey, speaking of Frost reminds me of something I had meant to ask you. How come you didn't get a specially trained dog, you know, to take you places?" he asked as they made their way along the slushy street. A chinook had blown in overnight and the temperatures had rocketed up to plus fourteen from minus twenty-five. Living in Calgary had its advantages.

"Actually, it's the humans who take the guide dogs places. These dogs cost thousands and thousands of bucks and take years to train. They're really great because they help their owners stay out of trouble when crossing the street or stop them from walking into walls or falling down stairs and tons of other things. They're really smart. It would also be neat to have a buddy who stayed with you all the time, but that's the way the dog cookie crumbles." He shrugged his shoulders as though it wasn't important, but Aiden heard the regret in his voice. "I have my name on a list for one, but so far, no pooch."

They were standing at the street waiting to cross, when Eric, his timing perfect, stepped into the street exactly when the crossing light changed, signalling they could walk. Again, Aiden wondered how Eric knew when the light had changed. "You drive me crazy when you do that. How do you know when to go?" he asked, hurrying to catch up.

Eric, wearing wild sunglasses that glowed fluorescent yellow, shook his head and sighed. "It's the same old story. Humans have five senses — taste, touch, smell, sound and sight. You sighted people rely on one sense way too much. Your motto should be *seeing is believing, the rest is baloney.* I can't *see* the light change, but I can *hear* it. Shut your eyes and listen," he instructed.

Aiden closed his eyes and listened. At first he didn't notice anything, then he heard it, a strange chirping sound. "That noise, that's how you do it! You can *hear* the signal change."

"Right again, Sherlock. Now shut up and keep listening." Eric was having a good time now.

Aiden did as he was told. Just as the light changed, signalling the other crosswalk to go, the noise changed. "The sound is different!" Aiden exclaimed.

"And he scores again! Each crosswalk direction has a different sound, east-west, one tone and north-south, a different one. When I hear the right tone, I know it's safe to cross." Eric continued walking toward the bus stop, his cane swinging jauntily in front of him.

Aiden was amazed when he thought of how many times he'd crossed streets and never noticed the noise, or if he did, never wondered what it was. He *saw* the signal and knew when to cross. It never occurred to him that there was any other way.

"Hey," Eric began, "are you doing anything next Friday night and could you help a friend in need? Only you can do this and it's very important." He waited for Aiden to answer.

"Ah, I don't think I'm doing anything, why? What's the favour, Runt?" Ever since the trip to the mall to buy underwear, Aiden was a little suspicious of Eric's plans.

"The Seeing Ice Dogs have an important game and we're short a player. We could really use another wicked skater on the team." He hesitated. "I know this is not the arrangement, but we could tell Michael this is in lieu of your Saturday visit, and then you'd have the whole weekend off." His voice sounded odd.

Aiden listened, really listened to Eric's voice, trying to use that sense to its fullest. Was that disappointment in Eric's voice? Was he worried that Aiden would jump at the chance to ditch him for a free Saturday? He'd have helped the Dogs out anyway, but he would love the chance to go over to his mom's on Saturday and stay overnight. That way, he and Frost could really get to know each other. It was perfect timing. Suddenly, Aiden thought of something even better.

"Look, let's get something straight." His tone was tough and he hid the smile in his voice. "I realize your wimpy wannabes could really use a star player like me and would do anything to get me to play, but…" He paused, then laughed. "I'll play because I want to, not because you think you can squirm out of seeing me on the weekend. There is a catch, though."

"Sure, you name it!" Eric said enthusiastically.

"*You* have to come with *me* on Saturday. Deal?" Aiden waited.

"Deal," Eric said in a very serious voice, but Aiden saw he was smiling.

11

A New Way of Seeing
Things

After Aiden cleared it with Michael, Kevin Gardner, the defenceman from the Ice Dogs, came to take him to the game on Friday. Aiden had forgotten to tell Charlie about playing, so he scribbled a note saying that he was at a hockey game and would be back later. He never said it was a Seeing Ice Dog game and that he'd be playing in it. He knew Charlie wouldn't like that.

Eric was waiting in Kevin's van. "You ready for this?" he asked.

"I was born ready," Aiden said, stowing his gear in the back of the SUV.

When the Seeing Ice Dogs had a game, the arena was usually packed and this Friday night was no exception. They were facing off against the Somerset Hornets. Aiden had never seen the Ice Dogs play in a real game, only practices.

He suited up wearing the red Seeing Ice Dog jersey. He had to admit it looked pretty sharp on. He and the other Ice Dogs were waiting in the players' box to start their warm-up when Kevin handed him a black helmet.

Aiden frowned. "I have my own," he said, tapping his white helmet.

Eric, waiting beside Aiden, suddenly looked guilty, or as guilty as you can look wearing rainbow-striped mirrored sunglasses and tiny skull and crossbones earrings. "Oh, yeah, Aiden, old buddy, pal," he began. "I forgot to tell you. We need you to play as a forward, so you have to wear a black helmet with customized goggles to make you technically blind," he finished up in a rush.

Aiden was confused. "What *customized goggles* to make me *technically blind*?" he asked suspiciously.

"It's like this," Eric explained. "We don't always have enough blind players to fill all the positions and we have to use these blacked-out goggles on sighted players so they can't see." He held his hands out and Kevin handed him the special goggles. "We paint the lenses black so the skater can't see. There are various simulations to duplicate the different types of visual impairment. Some are blacked out in the middle, leaving just the peripheral vision clear. Some have a small opening in the centre to simulate tunnel vision and some, like yours, are completely painted out to copy total blindness." He continued on. "The Hornets will be at a disadvantage because they'll have to field the same number of players with these special goggles as the Seeing Ice Dogs' blind skaters. The Hornets have no experience with playing blind, but for us, it's *all good*. We know just what to do."

"Why haven't I seen these before?" Aiden asked.

"We usually have enough blind players and I guess it never came up at practices. We use them in a real game because the other team is always 100 per cent sighted and we have to level the playing field." Eric handed Aiden the goggles. "There, that's all straightened out. Now, let's play hockey," he said as though that were the end of it.

Aiden looked down at the goggles. "You're crazy," he

scoffed. "I can't do this. To begin with, I'll look like an idiot." He was remembering how he felt the first time he played against the Seeing Ice Dogs. "And I have no clue how to play hockey without being able to see." He shook his head adamantly. "I can't do it; no one could!" He folded his arms across his chest.

Eric sighed. "I'm living proof it can be done, and so is Jeff Galbraith, Rod Rogalsky, Al Laughlin, Randy Cameron, Brian Clark and Gary Zarbock. We talked about this, how sighted people rely on one sense too much. Here's your chance to use those other senses we talked about. You know how to play slick hockey, Aiden. All you have to do is pretend you're doing it with your eyes closed. You can do this and we really need you." He held the goggles out.

Aiden thought about it. It was crazy. Then he looked out onto the ice and saw the Hornets taking their positions. He knew these guys were a regular team, but now several of them had different-coloured helmets, just like the Ice Dogs. The red and black helmeted players were wearing painted goggles. He glanced over at the goalie. He had a black helmet and goggles and was busily feeling around with his trapper and stick to find the edges of his net. Why weren't these guys worried about looking like idiots? Aiden tightened his grip on his stick. If they thought they were going to show him up, they had another thing coming. Reluctantly, he took the goggles from Eric's outstretched hands. "Let's play hockey," he grumbled, still not liking the idea.

The second he pulled the goggles and black helmet on he felt panic rise up and begin to choke him. He couldn't see a thing. His world had gone black.

"Come on, Aiden. I'll give you a tour of the rink." Eric's voice came to him from his left. He could hear the other players talking and laughing and the sensation was totally weird.

He started to step out of the players' box and forgot there was a short drop down to the ice. Pitching forward, he would have fallen except Eric heard him stumble and reached out to catch him.

Eric led him to the edge of the rink. "Just hold onto my arm while we skate a lap. There are a lot of things you do without stopping to think about it, like that first step," he said, chuckling. "Your brain would see something, automatically process how to handle it and let you go on. Now, you'll have to keep all that stuff in your head and play hockey, too. When it comes to playing the Ice Dogs, I feel sorry for the sighted guys. They don't know what's coming."

Aiden thought it was strange to feel sorry for the guys who *could* see. Didn't these blind guys understand how tough it was being unable to see a thing? He was having trouble just staying up on his skates. Even though he had skated his whole life, this felt totally new and strange to him. It was like he was learning to skate all over again.

The sounds of the other players whistling by him made him nervous. He could get creamed and never see the guy coming. He had to rely on the sighted players to warn him and the other blind skaters so they wouldn't take each other out. Aiden could feel sweat beading up on his forehead and would have flipped open his visor to wipe it, but he didn't want to let go of Eric's arm.

Eric began speaking. "Put your stick out and touch the boards. I'll take you around so you get a feel for how big the rink is and how different areas sound." He began leading Aiden around the ice. "Use your ears to position other skaters and you have to listen to what the sighted guys shout. They'll let you know what's coming — like a big defenceman or a backhand pass."

They made a couple of turns around the rink until Aiden thought he began to notice subtle changes in the sounds he heard. "Hey, I think I know when we're coming to a corner," he said, listening. "And when we're skating toward centre ice. The sounds have more echo." He was starting to get the feel of the ice beneath his skates, too.

Eric laughed, "Great, now you're getting the hang of it." They skated on, weaving in and out of players and around the goal.

"Hey, Rob, where are you?" Eric called to Rob Lane, the defenceman for the Ice Dogs.

"To your left, coming up from behind," the sighted D-man called.

"Pass me the puck so Aiden can hear how it sounds." Eric turned to pick up the pass.

Aiden listened hard. He heard Rob's stick connect with the metal puck and the rattling jangle as it sped toward them. "Got it," Eric called as the puck hit what Aiden assumed was the Runt's stick.

"Did you notice the change in sound as the puck came toward you?" Eric asked. "Timing is everything in this game. You have to know just when to reach out and snag the thing or you're chasing after a sound that's going away from you fast." They headed over to their players' box. "You're going to do great. There are some sighted players that can't even stay up on their skates when they put on the special goggles."

Aiden felt along the boards for the gate, then, remembering the step, made his way into the box. He pulled his helmet and goggles off and looked around. He'd never realized how much light there was in an arena before. "Okay, that was different." He wiped his forehead. He'd been concentrating so hard he was really sweating. "One thing, Runt," he said, putting his hand on

Eric's shoulder, "don't play me unless you have to. Compared to you guys, I stink."

The game turned out to be a lot of fun. The playing levels were higher than Aiden had thought they would be with slick stickhandling and speed the name of the game. When he was on the ice, he was not the best player out there, but he did listen well. He was soon able to tell approximately where the puck was by the direction of the noise. Once he was even able to intercept a pass and make a breakaway. Unfortunately, he'd become confused on the direction and had been heading for his own net.

"Turn around, Aiden. This isn't where you want to be!" Gary Zarbock called as he heard the puck getting closer.

Aiden had turned and headed back to the Hornets' end. He'd just crossed the blue line when he heard the swish of skates. "Who's there?" he called. "Randy? Kevin?"

"Not even close," the unfamiliar voice said. With a sudden jolt, Aiden was checked off the puck and sent spinning into the boards. He was unprepared and went down hard.

"You okay?" Ian Richardson called as he skated past.

"Yeah," Aiden said, climbing up the boards. "Just my ego is bruised." On the next line change, he pulled his helmet and goggles off, then sat next to Eric. Aiden looked around, amazed at how much he'd never noticed before.

"I heard you hit the boards," Eric said, taking a long drink from his water bottle. "How come you never creamed the guy?"

Aiden had to think about this for a moment. For some reason, the idea of grinding the guy into the ice had never occurred to him. It was a fair hit and fair hits were just a part of any hockey game. "I thought I'd wait for him in the parking lot later," he laughed, nudging Eric and causing him to pour water down the front of his jersey.

The game was in the last five minutes of the third period and the score was tied four all. Aiden watched the action closely. Gary really was an amazing goalie. He had some kind of sixth sense when it came to hockey.

"We sure would like to win this one," Al Laughlin said, shaking his head. "It's Gary's last game. His family is moving to Vancouver. Unfortunately, there's no blind hockey team there, so he won't be playing much."

Aiden looked at the fast goalie again. "Man, that sucks," was all he could think of to say. He knew Gary loved the game and to give it up would be terrible for him. It would be great if he could leave on a win. An idea started to come to Aiden. A play so crazy, no one would be able to stop it. Jumping up, he moved over to Randy and touched him on the arm. "We need to call a time out," he said excitedly. "I know how we can send Gary off with a win." When the Ice Dogs had gathered around, Aiden explained his idea.

"That sounds so wild, it just might work!" Rod Rogalsky said with a grin.

"I'm in!" Ian Richardson agreed.

"Let's go!" Aiden said as the Seeing Ice Dogs took to the ice with only two minutes left on the clock.

12

A Slick Play Saves the Day

Aiden knew his crazy play would work. The Ice Dogs took their places on the ice. Eric and Aiden would be forwards; Randy Cameron center; Danny Dawes and Kevin Gardner were defence, and Gary was between the pipes. Everything depended on timing. The clock was ticking and as it did the crowd grew noisier. Everyone was yelling for a win.

The action was frantic. The Hornets wanted this win as badly as the Ice Dogs and they weren't giving up. The crowd went wild as the tall Hornet centre intercepted an Ice Dog pass and turned to start his attack. As the centre closed in, both Hornet forwards set up close to the net. One of them would receive the pass and fire it in. Gary would have to figure out which one had the puck, prepare for the shot, and try to deflect it out past the other waiting forward.

"Okay, guys," Aiden called. "*Game on!*" These words were the signal that the winning play was about to begin.

Just then the Hornet forward on the right side of the crease lined up on the net and fired one at the lower corner.

The puck rattled toward the net and Aiden could hear Gary's big stick swing around on the ice.

With perfect timing, the Ice Dogs' goalie deflected the puck, sending it back out to the far left, where Eric stood waiting. "I'm here, Gary!" he called loudly.

The puck hit his stick with a clean smack. The Hornet players began swarming toward Eric, ready to strip the puck from him and pepper Gary again.

As the Hornets closed in on Eric, instead of turning for the Hornet end as everyone anticipated, he almost casually slid the puck back to Gary, then he turned and headed down ice.

Expertly snagging the puck, Gary then snapped it back out to Randy, who had been quietly waiting on the right side of the goal crease. Randy turned and flipped a pass to Kevin, who was waiting just this side of the blue line. The second the spinning metal puck hit his stick, Kevin headed toward the Hornet goal with Aiden and Eric close behind him.

They crossed the centre line, and were going for the Hornets' blue line when Kevin passed across ice to Aiden who, playing as a blind forward, could take it in to score.

Aiden heard, rather than saw, the puck on his stick. The crucial shot would have to be fast and on target and they would have only one try at it before the rest of the Hornet swarm arrived. "I'm not sure I can get one past this guy and it's our last chance. You take it in, Runt!" Aiden called as they crossed into Hornet territory.

"No way! You earned this, Aiden! You can do it!" Eric yelled back.

Aiden knew they had to be fast or the play wouldn't work. He began cutting toward the net. The Hornet goalie was a big guy and would be even more impressive in his bulky pads. It would be tricky to get one past him.

Using all the skating expertise he'd learned, Aiden concentrated on his timing and puck control as he jangled the metal puck across the front of the goalmouth.

The noise of the puck had the goggle-wearing goalie

disoriented as he tried to get a fix on where Aiden would attack. Aiden could hear him hitting the goalposts with his stick as he defended the open net.

Stopping dead still in front of the goal, Aiden listened to all the sounds in the rink. He heard the swish of the players' skates on the ice as they headed toward him. He also heard hockey sticks scraping along the ice and the crowd yelling.

He concentrated harder. Then he heard his own raspy breathing and the thudding of his pounding heart. He also heard the goalie moving across the goalmouth as he followed the noisy puck. Aiden waited until he was sure the goalie had moved to the far side of the net, then he grabbed the puck back onto his stick and fired a sizzler into what he hoped was the undefended open corner.

Aiden held his breath, listening, hoping the puck had really gone in. Could he have missed the open net entirely?

Then everything happened at once. The goal light whirled; the crowd cheered, and the buzzer sounded ending the game. The Seeing Ice Dogs poured onto the ice, pulling Gary out of his goal and congratulating him on his slick puck-handling and the coolest win of the season.

Pulling his helmet and goggles off, Aiden glided over to Eric, put out his arm and guided the youngest Ice Dog down to the noisy crowd of hockey players. "Come on, Runt. I'll escort you to the victory celebrations!" As soon as the two boys skated up, everyone began cheering Aiden for not only coming up with the slickest play of the game, but also making it look so easy. He was overwhelmed by his teammates' enthusiasm.

Gary patted him on his helmet. "Not bad for a rookie. I wish I was going to be here to see what you come up with next!" The goalie's voice was full of regret.

"A smart guy like you should be able to start a blind hockey team in Vancouver," Aiden said. "After all, the Seeing Ice Dogs could use some competition!"

Gary smiled and nodded. "Just give me a few months and you're on!"

It was a game to remember and Aiden would. He had never felt more like part of a team or happier in his life.

* * *

Aiden raced into the house, not bothering to strip off his winter boots. "Charlie! Charlie! You'll never guess what happened at the game tonight!"

Charlie sat in his recliner in the living room. Dim light glowed from one small lamp in the corner. "Where have you been, boy?" His voice was like stone.

Aiden stopped in his tracks. He'd heard that tone before. His throat felt tight as he tried to swallow. "I...I was at a hockey game," he stammered.

"I checked the schedule. There was no Devil game tonight. I don't like being lied to, so I'll ask you again. *Where were you, boy?*" He stood up and slowly moved toward Aiden.

Aiden took an involuntary step backward, his hand reaching instinctively for the birthmark on his neck. "I was at a hockey game, like I said in my note." He realized he had about two seconds to explain before Charlie stopped listening. "It was a Seeing Ice Dogs' game. They were short a player so I filled in. I left you a note!" His voice had a note of desperation in it and he knew Charlie had heard it.

A twisted sneer spread across Charlie's face. "You were playing with those losers? I thought we had an understanding about what's real hockey and what's not? You wasted a Friday night with those freaks when you could have been home with your old man?"

Aiden looked around, feeling like a cornered animal. "I phoned Michael and he said it was okay. I just switched my Saturday time with Eric and spent it with him tonight. That way I don't have to see him tomorrow and I can stay home with you." He thought about his plans to take Eric to see Frost. That would just have to wait until next week.

Charlie's eyes narrowed, and then he nodded his head. "Then you can consider your time with the blind kid as done. That Long Feather jerk came over tonight with the papers that said your community service is over. You're off the hook. No more Eric or his wimp hockey team. You can concentrate on getting your reputation as an enforcer back."

Aiden couldn't believe what he'd heard. He'd been enjoying himself so much lately, he'd forgotten his community service was supposed to end at Christmas. "Oh, man! I forgot."

"Yeah, you can forget this whole thing now and get back to normal. And as for me," he said, taking a step toward Aiden. "I don't want to hear one more word about that blind kid or his nowhere team. It's over. *Do you understand?*"

Aiden nodded his head. The future stretched out in front of him just the way it used to be before all of this had happened. His stomach gave a lurch...*just the way it used to be.*

He turned and went to his room, feeling numb. He'd been shopping and looked at the pile of Christmas presents stacked neatly on his desk in the corner. He'd used his paper route money to buy the gifts. It hit him like a ton of bricks just how much he was going to miss Eric and the Seeing Ice Dogs and even Michael. He'd been a good listener when Aiden had needed an adult ear. He remembered how excited he was about taking Eric to his mom's to meet Frost. That wouldn't happen now. A lot of things wouldn't happen now — like ever playing with the Seeing Ice Dogs again and hanging out with Eric.

Walking over to his desk, Aiden picked up the cartridge pack for the GameBox he'd bought himself. It had taken all the rest of his money and left him broke, but it had all the wickedest games and had been in such big demand; his had been the last one in the store. The clerk had said he probably had the only one left in the whole city. Aiden had really been looking forward to trying them out. He hefted the box in his hand. Some other kid was going to have a great Christmas after Aiden went back to the mall tomorrow.

*   *   *

Aiden had called Michael and asked to meet with him. Saturday morning, Aiden left for the mall where he and Michael would meet. He finished everything he had to do, then met the probation officer at the food court.

"Charlie told me the news last night," Aiden said, taking a bite out of his burger.

"You passed with flying colours. You've proved you can control your temper and I don't think I'll be seeing you in the future." Michael smiled at him. "I had my doubts in the beginning, but you showed me you were able to overcome some basic behavioural problems that I don't think were entirely your fault." He took a sip of his iced tea. "You, Charlie and your mom should consider family counselling and your dad should also have anger management courses. Has he ever mentioned taking anything like that?"

Aiden just stared at him like he was from Mars. "Are you kidding? That mumbo jumbo is for chumps. Charlie says there's nothing wrong with him or me. It's the other losers who have the problem."

"After everything that's happened, do you still think Charlie's right about that?" Michael looked at Aiden, who suddenly found it hard to swallow.

"Look, Charlie's okay. He just does things more directly than other dads. If someone jerks his chain, he straightens them out right away." Aiden put his burger down on the wrapper. His appetite had disappeared.

"I want you to think about how things have been lately and how things are going to be from now on. You can't change the past, but you can help choose your future. *If* you continue to learn, not just from your mistakes and failures but from your successes, too." He pushed his empty glass away. "Just think about it." He started to get up, then stopped. "Oh, and Aiden, don't lose my phone number. If you ever need me, just call."

They were going to go to the arena where the Seeing Ice Dogs were practising so Aiden could say goodbye to Eric. He hadn't known that the game against the Hornets would be the last time he saw the runt.

13

A Second Chance

The Seeing Ice Dogs had finished practice and were filing into the dressing room when they arrived. "Hey, Runt!" Aiden called as he spotted the small hockey player. Today he had on blue corduroy pants with a yellow turtleneck and red suspenders with penguins. His sunglasses were white and patriotically decorated with small red maple leafs.

"Hey, Aiden! How's it hanging, bro?" His big Chiclet teeth filled his wide grin. "I didn't think I'd see you again after Michael called with the good news."

Aiden wasn't sure finishing his community service was *good news*. "I just wanted to stop by and well, actually…" He felt like an idiot and wasn't sure how to say what he wanted to say.

Eric shook his head. "You wanted to tell me what a blast you've had and you'd like to continue to be my buddy. No sweat! In fact, I was thinking the same thing."

"Would that be allowed, Michael?" Aiden looked at the probation officer.

Michael nodded. "I think the judge would make an exception."

"I wasn't sure I'd be able to see you again, so I brought your Christmas present with me. You can open it now if you want." Aiden reached out and took Eric's hand, placing a gift-wrapped package into it.

"No way! You goof, you shouldn't have!" Eric said, feeling the bow on the present before ripping the paper open. He pulled the red, white and blue shirt out and held it up.

"It's a New York Rangers' jersey with Eric Lindros's name and number eighty-eight on the back," Aiden explained. "I know he's your hero and everyone needs a hero." He punched Eric on the shoulder gently. "Even a runt like you."

Eric traced the name and number with his fingers. "I've always wanted one. I don't know what to say."

"Well, that's a first," Michael laughed.

Just then, the dressing room door burst open and Charlie came storming in. Everyone stopped and stared. His face was red and his eyes were filled with rage.

"I told you, we were done with all this, boy!" he snarled as he grabbed Aiden by the collar.

Aiden was so surprised, he couldn't say a word.

"Take it easy, Charlie," Michael said calmly, trying to defuse the situation. "Aiden just came to give Eric his Christmas present."

Charlie glanced at the jersey Eric was holding. "As if you even know what this is!" Reaching out with his big hand, he jerked the shirt violently out of the young boy's grasp with such force that Eric went sprawling across the floor, his brightly coloured sunglasses flying off his face.

Eric looked up toward Aiden with strange sightless eyes. Aiden had never seen Eric without his sunglasses and he was startled at how the boy looked.

Eric seemed to shrink before Aiden's eyes. He suddenly looked helpless and vulnerable. Eric started frantically feeling around for his sunglasses. "Can you help me find my glasses?" he pleaded in a small voice. "Please, will someone help me find my glasses," he whimpered. His voice was filled with fear as though without his trademark cool lenses, the world would see that he was just a young blind boy who needed help.

Charlie stared down at the helpless boy, revulsion on his face.

Michael quickly stepped between Eric and Charlie. "*That's enough!*" he said loudly, with more authority than Aiden had ever heard before. The force in his voice tore Charlie's gaze away from Eric. "The jersey is Eric's property and I'll take it for him." He reached out for the shirt.

Dropping the jersey on the floor, Charlie turned on Michael, grabbing him in his huge hands and viciously slamming the probation officer against the wall. "You no good interfering Indian…"

As Aiden watched, terrified, Charlie's iron fist came back ready to drive into Michael's face.

"Stop!" Aiden heard himself scream. "Stop it, Charlie!" He ran between his dad and Michael, as tears suddenly began streaming down his face. "Stop it! Stop it! *Stop it!*" he shouted, as his dad pushed on the man with all his might.

Charlie stared at his son, not believing what he saw.

Aiden couldn't control his crying now. His heart was thudding in his ears, but he couldn't help himself. "Please, Dad, just stop it." His voice was a choked sob.

Charlie looked at his son first with disgust, then with confusion. "What's happened to you, boy? I didn't raise you to be a snivelling little whiner."

Aiden wiped at his face. His hand automatically started to cover the birthmark on his neck; then he stopped, lowered his hands and raised his chin instead. The words came spilling out as though a dam had burst. "No, you didn't Charlie. But I can't be that boy anymore." His voice dropped to a whisper. "Don't you see? I don't *want* to be that boy anymore." He backed away from his father. "I like me now. I like not having to beat every kid up who even looks at me wrong. I like having friends." He shook his head. "And I know you'll never understand, but this is how it's got to be. This is how *I've* got to be if I'm ever going to be happy because I don't want to go through life hating me…or you."

Charlie's eyes narrowed and he pointed a finger at Aiden. "You don't know what you're talking about, boy. You need to be straightened out!" But his finger trembled as he said it and both Aiden and his dad saw it shake. Suddenly, the big man spun around and strode out of the dressing room without a backward glance.

Aiden watched him leave and somehow, he didn't look as big or tough as he used to. Instead, he just looked sad.

Aiden walked over and helped Eric to his feet; then, reaching down, picked up his friend's glasses and gently placed them back on the blind boy's face. One lens was cracked, but it was barely noticeable. "You okay, Runt?"

Eric slowly nodded his head. "No worries." He tried to sound brave, but Aiden saw his lip quiver.

Michael dusted off the hockey jersey that had fallen onto the floor and handed it to Eric. "I believe this is yours, Eric." Then he turned to Aiden. "What do you want to do now?" he asked, his face full of concern.

Aiden thought about everything that had happened over the past three months. His life had changed; *he* had changed and he hadn't even realized it. What he'd said to his dad was the truth. He did like the person he was now and he knew he could never go back to the way he was. "I think I should go over to my mom's house. She's always talked about how much she wants me to come and live with her. Maybe we could see if that would be possible." He suddenly felt very tired. "Could you give me a ride and maybe talk to her with me? Explain things?" he asked Michael hopefully.

Michael smiled and nodded. "You bet. I have to put recommendations into my final report to the judge and I may be adding a couple."

Eric readjusted his glasses. "Do you still want to get together on Saturdays?" Eric asked, his voice sounding a little unsure.

Aiden reached out and put his hand on his friend's shoulder. "My weekends wouldn't be the same if I didn't hang out with you, Eric." His throat suddenly felt tight and he cleared it self-consciously. "As your best friend, I have to help a runt like you find out how *we* can go to that blind hockey camp you were telling me about. If they can play any kind of quality hockey at all, you'll need my coaching just to get on the team!" he laughed. "And then I want you to come over to my mom's and meet a small furry friend."

He nudged Eric gently with his elbow. With his new friend holding on to his arm, the two boys walked out of the dressing room together.

14

A Goal in Sight

It had been nearly two months since the incident in the dressing room and Aiden couldn't believe how his life had changed.

He looked around his new room at his mom's. He and Michael had spent a whole Saturday at the mall shopping for hockey posters to decorate the pale blue walls. Eric had helped and had even given him one of his special autographed posters to hang over his bed.

"Aiden, come on, honey. Eric and Michael are here." His mom poked her head around the door of his room and smiled at him.

She looked somehow younger since the judge had allowed Aiden to move in with her. The worry lines she always had were gone and she hummed a lot. "Just finishing packing, Mom." He stuffed the last of his hockey gear into his equipment bag.

Just then, Frost bounded into the room and onto the bed. The frisky pup had one of Aiden's big hockey socks hanging out of his mouth and obviously wanted to play tug-of-war.

"Not now, Frost. Eric will be here in a minute and you can play all you want." Aiden and Eric were going to the hockey camp and Michael was driving them both there.

The doorbell rang and Frost sprang off the bed and began

racing downstairs, barking wildly, but still managing to hold onto the sock with his teeth.

Aiden grabbed his bags and followed his dog and mom downstairs.

"You ready to go?" Eric asked as soon as he was inside the door.

"Where did you find those? They're the weirdest ones yet!" Aiden laughed, staring at Eric's newest sunglasses.

"You like?" Eric asked, tipping his head this way and that so Aiden could get the full effect. The glasses were painted in NHL colours and the image of a hockey puck with the NHL logo on it was reflected in the mirrored lenses. "Aren't they the best!"

"Oh, those are doozies all right!" Aiden agreed as he rolled his eyes.

"Great! I'm glad you like them because I got you a pair, too!" Eric held out his hand and presented Aiden with a matching pair of flashy sunglasses.

Instead of saying that they were too geeky to wear, Aiden took the glasses and slipped them on. "Hey, these are cool! Thanks, Runt." He grinned and patted Eric's shoulder. A couple of months ago, he would have thought nothing of telling a kid like Eric just how ridiculous the glasses looked, but now, he would never have hurt his best friend's feelings.

Michael smiled in approval. "You two dudes are going to be the best-looking rookies at hockey camp."

Aiden's mom looked at Michael and something in her eyes made Aiden do a double take.

Come to think of it, Michael had been over to the house a lot lately. The quiet probation officer had also gone with them to the movies twice and been to Sunday dinner several weeks in a row. This made Aiden feel surprisingly good. He loved his mom and liked seeing her happy. Michael wasn't such a bad guy either.

"My parents almost changed their minds about letting me go," Eric said, feeling in his pocket. "So my mom made me bring these, just in case." He held up a new jumbo pack of batteries. There must have been twenty in the bubble-wrapped package.

"What are they for?" Aiden asked, wondering why his friend would possibly need twenty batteries.

Eric laughed and pulled out his cell phone. "I didn't have the heart to tell her it doesn't use those kind of batteries. I figure she'll sleep better at night if she thinks my phone will always be charged up."

They all laughed and began hauling Aiden's gear out to Michael's car. Eric led the way with his cane tapping the sidewalk and Frost trying to grab it as it swayed back and forth.

Aiden's mom put her arm around her son's shoulder. "I got a call from your dad last night."

Aiden immediately tensed, but his mom squeezed his shoulder and smiled at him reassuringly. "He called to say he's going to an anger management class and was wondering if we wanted to go to family counselling with him." She looked down at her son. "I said we would have to discuss it. I don't want you to feel any pressure, Aiden, but it might do us all good to talk about…" She hesitated and her smooth brow creased into a frown. "Things."

Aiden thought about everything that had happened. He and Michael had talked about how Aiden felt and his ex-probation officer and newest friend had helped him understand a lot of his feelings. Things didn't bother him like they used to. He didn't need to use his fists to show everyone how tough he was. He'd even made some friends at school and his grades had come up.

Aiden felt much stronger about himself now and the idea of making things better between him and his dad didn't seem so impossible anymore. It would be great if they could get along as a family, even a family who lived in different houses.

"Sure, Mom." He tried to sound casual, but his voice quavered just a little. It was a big step and they both knew it. "When I get back from camp, we should set something up."

It was his turn to smile reassuringly at his mom. After all, everyone needs something to shoot for. It's important to have a goal in sight.

Other books you'll enjoy in the Sports Stories series...

Baseball

❏ *Curve Ball* by John Danakas #1
Tom Poulos is looking forward to a summer of baseball in Toronto
until his mother puts him on a plane to Winnipeg.

❏ *Baseball Crazy* by Martyn Godfrey #10
Rob Carter wins an all-expenses-paid chance to be bat boy at the
Blue Jays spring training camp in Florida.

❏ *Shark Attack* by Judi Peers #25
The East City Sharks have a good chance of winning the county
championship until their arch rivals get a tough new pitcher.

❏ *Hit and Run* by Dawn Hunter and Karen Hunter #35
Glen Thomson is a talented pitcher, but as his ego inflates, team
morale plummets. Will he learn from being benched for losing his
temper?

❏ *Power Hitter* by C. A. Forsyth #41
Connor's summer was looking like a write-off. That is, until he discovered his secret talent.

❏ *Sayonara, Sharks* by Judi Peers #48
In this sequel to Shark Attack, Ben and Kate are excited about the
school trip to Japan, but Matt's not sure he wants to go.

Basketball

❏ *Fast Break* by Michael Coldwell #8
Moving from Toronto to small-town Nova Scotia was rough, but
when Jeff makes the school basketball team he thinks things are
looking up.

❏ *Camp All-Star* by Michael Coldwell #12
In this insider's view of a basketball camp, Jeff Lang encounters
some unexpected challenges.

❏ *Nothing but Net* by Michael Coldwell #18
The Cape Breton Grizzly Bears prepare for an out-of-town basketball tournament they're sure to lose.

❏ *Slam Dunk* by Steven Barwin and Gabriel David Tick #23
In this sequel to Roller Hockey Blues, Mason Ashbury's basketball
team adjusts to the arrival of some new players: girls.

Figure Skating

Gymnastics

❏ *The Perfect Gymnast* by Michele Martin Bossley #9
Abby's new friend has all the confidence she needs, but she also has
a serious problem that nobody but Abby seems to know about.
sort things out?

Ice Hockey

❏ *Two Minutes for Roughing* by Joseph Romain #2
As a new player on a tough Toronto hockey team, Les must fight to
fit in.

❏ *Hockey Night in Transcona* by John Danakas #7
Cody Powell gets promoted to the Transcona Sharks' first line,
bumping out the coach's son, who's not happy with the change.

❏ *Face Off* by C. A. Forsyth #13
A talented hockey player finds himself competing with his best
friend for a spot on a select team.

❏ *Hat Trick* by Jacqueline Guest #20
The only girl on an all-boy hockey team works to earn the captain's
respect and her mother's approval.

❏ *Hockey Heroes* by John Danakas #22
A left-winger on the thirteen-year-old Transcona Sharks adjusts to a
new best friend and his mom's boyfriend.

❏ *Hockey Heat Wave* by C. A. Forsyth #27
In this sequel to Face Off, Zack and Mitch run into trouble when it
looks as if only one of them will make the select team at hockey
camp.

❏ *Shoot to Score* by Sandra Richmond #31
Playing defense on the B list alongside the coach's mean-spirited son
is a tough obstacle for Steven to overcome, but he perseveres and
changes his luck.

❏ *Rookie Season* by Jacqueline Guest #42
What happens when a boy wants to join an all-girl hockey team?

❏ *Brothers on Ice* by John Danakas #44
Brothers Dylan and Deke both want to play goal for the same team.

❏ *Rink Rivals* by Jacqueline Guest #49
A move to Calgary finds the Evans twins pitted against each other on
the ice, and struggling to help each other out of trouble.

❑ *Power Play* by Michele Martin Bossley #50
An early-season injury causes Zach Thomas to play timidly, and a
school bully just makes matters worse. Will a famous hockey player
will be able to help Zach sort things out?

Riding

❑ *A Way with Horses* by Peter McPhee #11
A young Alberta rider, invited to study show jumping at a posh local
riding school, uncovers a secret.

❑ *Riding Scared* by Marion Crook #15
A reluctant new rider struggles to overcome her fear of horses.

❑ *Katie's Midnight Ride* by C. A. Forsyth #16
An ambitious barrel racer finds herself without a horse weeks before
her biggest rodeo.

❑ *Glory Ride* by Tamara L. Williams #21
Chloe Anderson fights memories of a tragic fall for a place on the
Ontario Young Riders Team.

❑ *Cutting It Close* by Marion Crook #24
In this novel about barrel racing, a young rider finds her horse is in
trouble just as she's about to compete in an important event.

❑ *Shadow Ride* by Tamara L. Williams #37
Bronwen has to choose between competing aggressively for herself
or helping out a teammate.

Roller Hockey

❑ *Roller Hockey Blues* by Steven Barwin and Gabriel David
Tick #17
Mason Ashbury faces a summer of boredom until he makes the roller
hockey team.

Sailing

❑ *Sink or Swim* by William Pasnak #5
Dario can barely manage the dog paddle, but thanks to his mother
he's spending the summer at a water sports camp.

Soccer

❏ *Lizzie's Soccer Showdown* by John Danakas #3
When Lizzie asks why the boys and girls can't play together, she finds herself the new captain of the soccer team.

❏ *Alecia's Challenge* by Sandra Diersch #32
Thirteen-year-old Alecia has to cope with a new school, a new step-father, and friends who have suddenly discovered the opposite sex.

❏ *Shut-Out!* by Camilla Reghelini Rivers #39
David wants to play soccer more than anything, but will the new coach let him?

❏ *Offside!* by Sandra Diersch #43
Alecia has to confront a new girl who drives her teammates crazy.

❏ *Heads Up!* by Dawn Hunter and Karen Hunter #45
Do the Warriors really need a new, hot-shot player who skips practice?

❏ *Off the Wall* by Camilla Reghelini Rivers #52
Lizzie loves indoor soccer, and she's thrilled when her little sister gets into the sport. But when their teams are pitted against each other, Lizzie can only warn her sister to watch out.

❏ *Trapped!* by Michele Martin Bossley #53
There's a thief on Jane's soccer team, and everyone thinks it's her best friend, Ashley. Jane must find the true culprit to save both Ashley and the team's morale.

Swimming

❏ *Breathing Not Required* by Michele Martin Bossley #4
Gracie works so hard to be chosen for the solo at synchronized swimming that she almost loses her best friend in the process.

❏ *Water Fight!* by Michele Martin Bossley #14
Josie's perfect sister is driving her crazy, but when she takes up swimming — Josie's sport — it's too much to take.

❏ *Taking a Dive* by Michele Martin Bossley #19
Josie holds the provincial record for the butterfly, but in this sequel to Water Fight! she can't seem to match her own time and might not go on to the nationals.

❏ *Great Lengths* by Sandra Diersch #26
Fourteen-year-old Jessie decides to find out whether the rumours about a new swimmer at her Vancouver club are true.

❑ *Pool Princess* by Michele Martin Bossley #47
In this sequel to Breathing Not Required, Gracie must deal with a
bully on the new synchro team in Calgary.

Track and Field

❑ *Mikayla's Victory* by Cynthia Bates #29
Mikayla must compete against her friend if she wants to represent
her school at an important track event.

❑ *Fast Finish* by Bill Swan #30
Noah is a promising young runner headed for the provincial finals
when he suddenly decides to withdraw from the event.

❑ *Walker's Runners* by Robert Rayner #55
Toby Morton hates gym. In fact, he doesn't run for anything —
except the classroom door. Then Mr. Walker arrives and persuades
Toby to join the running team.